THE KEY

Susan Wicks grew up in Kent and studied French at the universities of Hull and Sussex, where she wrote a Ph.D. thesis on the fiction of André Gide. She has taught in France and at University College, Dublin. She is author of three collections of poetry, the latest of which, *The Clever Daughter*, was a Poetry Book Society Choice, and a prose memoir, *Driving My Father*. Her second novel, *Little Thing*, was published in 1998. She now lives with her husband and two daughters in Tunbridge Wells, and works as a part-time tutor for the University of Kent.

by the same author

poetry

SINGING UNDERWATER
OPEN DIAGNOSIS
THE CLEVER DAUGHTER

prose

DRIVING MY FATHER

fiction

THE KEY
LITTLE THING

The Key

SUSAN WICKS

for Victoria
with admiration and
very best wishes
for your own writing,

Susan Wicks

Totleigh Barton
Nov. 03.

ff

faber and faber

LONDON · BOSTON

First published in 1997
by Faber and Faber Limited
3 Queen Square London WC1N 3AU

Phototypeset by Intype London Ltd.
Printed and bound in Great Britain by
Mackays of Chatham PLC, Chatham, Kent

A CIP record for this book
is available from the British Library

ISBN 0-571-19203-3

2 4 6 8 10 9 7 5 3 1

A man who reads a marriage advertisement newspaper can set free, one by one, several of the men that exist inside himself: the man who lusts, the man who thinks; in that 'man who thinks' there is also a man who is weeping.

Montherlant, *Young Girls*

The madrigal is perhaps the most satisfying form of music ever derived for recreational singing.

Simon Carrington

CHAPTER 1

JANE, 37, 5ft 7in, attractive, gsoh, honest and sincere, wltm an attractive male, tall, 35–45, for friendship, possible relationship.

PHILOSOPHICAL MALE, intelligent, profound, stimulating company, many interests, enjoys good conversation, seeks adaptable, attractive, well-spoken/ educated female of similar age.

BUBBLY 43-YR-OLD female wltm wonderful male to enjoy all of life's good things together. Really missing a cuddle from an affectionate partner.

LARGE WICKER TOY basket, as new £15.

BEAUTIFUL GARDEN STONEWARE. Make your own with our high quality fibreglass moulds. Urns, bird baths, gnomes, etc. Make at least 500% or more profit. Ask us how. Send for our special starter pack now.

THOUGHTFUL, GENUINE man sought by not unattractive, 30-year-old single parent, initially for friendship.

TARANTULAS, VARIOUS SPECIES incl. **huge and beautiful** bird-eaters. Call Mike for list with free full-colour Goliath bird-eater photo.

My friend Deborah entered a competition once. For one of those highbrow papers, I think it was. I don't know how she did it. I think she actually won.

'What did you have to do?' I asked her.

'Well.' She frowned, chewing the end of her pencil. 'It was for a small ad. One of those personal things. It wasn't really that difficult. You had to use all the letters of the alphabet.'

'Like the quick brown fox?' I said.

She looked at me. 'No. Not like the quick brown fox. Just the initial letters. Active backpacker / camper desires . . .'

' . . . elephantine footloose grandfather?'

She snorted. 'Something like that.'

I thought about it. 'And did it work? Did they print it?'

'Oh, yes. They printed it. That was part of the prize. And it worked . . . up to a point.' She sighed. Then she laughed. 'We had some good times. He taught me about Beethoven's late quartets. And we went to bed. I hadn't been to bed with anyone for about ten years.'

Suddenly I found myself getting interested. 'And what was he like?'

'Like an elephantine footloose grandfather,' she said.

I turn my key in the lock and the cottage door swings open. The little front room is in darkness, empty except for the usual litter of papers. I turn on the light. There is a dirty glass on the low table by the fireplace. On the mat there is a letter from Annie.

France. French paper. French stamps. I pick it up and turn it over in my hand. Then I stick my thumb under the flap and tear it open. *Mum, it's great here. I love it. But I decided to come home for Christmas, see you and Laura, if she's around. Can I bring you something back (other than my dirty laundry!!!)? Xav's going* to *Mégèves (is that how you spell it???) for a fortnight, and he wanted me to go with him but I don't know, I think for Christmas I'd rather come home and see you. Not that I'm missing you, or home, or anything (ha!). But anyway if it's okay by you I thought I'd come. Is that alright? Let me know if it isn't.* I fold up the double sheet of squared paper and put it back in the envelope. Christmas is a long way away.

There is a free newspaper too. I've left my footprint right across the front page. I pick it up and carry it with me to the kitchen. But there is nothing in it. It is only full of advertisements. I spread it out on the kitchen table and use it to catch the drips from my cup of tea.

'BUBBLY 43-YR-OLD . . .' I try to picture her, the woman who has composed this advertisement. She has spent a whole evening searching for just the right words, and now the tea bleeds into the paper, making it half illegible. I try to imagine the kind of replies she will get. I circle her ad with a neat halo of red ink. Then I get the kitchen scissors and cut it out. Now I can carry it around in my pocket. Whenever I feel like re-reading it, I can get it out. If I'm bending to unlock my car in the rain and a passing lorry drives through a puddle and covers my legs with brown graffiti, I shall be able to reach for the slip of paper and unfold it. I shall smooth out the creases against the palm of my hand. I can read and re-read it, under my breath, holding her words in my lungs for a moment and letting them out slowly.

What kind of woman describes herself as 'bubbly'? I try to imagine it. I go into the bathroom and look at myself in the mirror. I look ordinary, solid and flat and rather dull. I pout slightly and my image pouts back at me. I pull a strand of hair forward across my cheek and pout through it. Then I pull it across my upper lip and scrunch up my mouth to hold it there, like a greying moustache.

But when I go to bed she is still with me. Pouting. Bubbly. It is difficult to get to sleep. I try to empty my mind of her and think of something more reassuring. But she is there, somewhere in the room. *Really missing a cuddle.* I touch myself cautiously under the bedclothes. I am still there. Neither missing nor really missing. I ask myself what the difference is.

I am kneeling on the floor in the back room of the shop to unpack the boxes of new books. I am still thinking of her. The nylon tape resists me. The staples are heavy-duty. I look up to scan the desk for a pair of scissors.

Oliver is sitting there, hunched over the computer-screen. 'Are the scissors anywhere around?' I ask him.

He grunts. I hear him tap a key.

'Scissors?' I say again.

He hands them to me over his shoulder, his fair stubble greenish in the light from the VDU, his earring glittering. Then he turns away from me again. I hear the keys clicking.

'I'm not sure these are going to be sharp enough to slit my wrists,' I say.

'You're looking different today. I can't put my finger on what it is.' Deborah stops eating to study me, her fork suspended in mid-air, a wisp of curly lettuce dangling.

'It's the lipstick. I never wear it usually.'

'Yes.' She looks doubtful. 'That could be it. Or maybe something else.'

I take a big bite of my toasted sandwich. 'Like what?'

'I don't know. It *is* something about your mouth. Not the lipstick, though. More sort of the way you're holding it. Are you okay? Has something happened? Have you just been to the dentist?'

'Or perhaps it's the mood I'm in.' I tilt my head and flick my hair back.

'What mood are you in?'

'I don't know really. Miserable. Sort of . . . bubbly,' I say.

Perhaps she is right. As I drive back along the lanes I test my

5

teeth carefully with my tongue, one by one. I dislodge a poppy-seed and spit it out on to my finger, a small wet bubble of black like caviare. I shake my hand hard. Around me, from the nearby fields, gulls fly up noisily, showing the undersides of their wings.

I am trying to remember how I first met Devlan.

I am trying to remember.

And at first all that rises is his voice, and a sick gasp in the pit of my stomach like impotence or shame.

His voice. He had different voices, quite distinct pitches and intonations for different situations. If he had come into the world with a ventriloquist's dummy on his knee, I wouldn't have been surprised.

But that first time there was no dummy. He had asked me to go with him for a cup of coffee. We left the building and made our way into a crowded arcade just off the High Street. I followed him to Seeley's, upstairs, the table by the balustrade overlooking the ground floor. I sipped my coffee slowly. Below us a man with a bald head was laughing. A young woman was bending over to strap a toddler into a pushchair. And his voice surrounded me, a single male voice, without echoes or unnatural harmonies. 'The trouble with all this learning . . .' Devlan said. He was stirring the coffee in his cup, looking thoughtful.

'I thought you believed in it?'

'Oh, I do. Of course I do. It expands horizons. Every year the women come and enrol, and every year I see them change and grow.'

'So what's wrong with that?'

'Nothing. That's what it's all about. Change. Growth.'

'But . . .?'

'But the trouble is they change too fast. They risk growing into something they can't handle.'

'What do you mean?'

6

'I mean if they're not careful they grow out of their husbands,' Devlan said.

Raise your right shoulder four times. Now the left. Roll them back slowly. Reach up for four. Punch in front of you, keep your hips still, let your shoulders go with it. Twist and punch. KEEP YOUR HIPS STILL. Now reach sideways for four. Now on the left. Now reach up in the middle. Monkey plié. Lunge and stretch. Reach forwards. Open your chest. Extend the left foot, turn your toe to the mirror. DON'T LET THAT RIGHT KNEE ROLL IN. Curl up. And toe-taps. On the right. Now on the left. Now extend that right foot backwards. KEEP YOUR TOE STRAIGHT. Now bring it in and sit back on it, stretch that muscle just above the ankle. Hands on the right leg, extend the left. AND recover. HOLD THE ANKLE, NOT THE TOE. LOOK AT SOMETHING STRAIGHT AHEAD OF YOU.

I look straight ahead of me. Beyond the blur of bodies, my own, in the mirror, looking sheepish. The woman in front of me is immensely tall, her brown back criss-crossed with complicated straps like thongs, her blond bob bouncing over her shoulders. Behind her in my rainbow T-shirt I look like a garden gnome.

Now get ready to tap the step with your toes for eight. Bicep curls. Now heels, bow and arrow arms. Now fours. Now twos. Now SINGLES.

The rush of blood begins to spread a grin over our faces as we relax into the familiar routine. The whole class is half smiling now, the singles containing us in their synchronic pattern, precise and stylised. We are like majorettes or mechanical soldiers, all identical and visually pleasing, each of us justified by the others. Yet each of us is capable of making a mistake, of spoiling the pattern. You only have to lose concentration for a moment, to be tired or thirsty. Or a drop of sweat runs down into your eye. You blink and shake your head. But by the time you can see clearly again, the music has moved on.

*

Devlan's voices. The boyish, enthusiastic voice, that laughed when he laughed. The serious voice, several tones lower. The quiet, angry voice. The bland, colourless voice of the doctor you force to tell you you're going to die.

And there were also the silences. After he spoke, or after I spoke. Perhaps there were more of those than anything.

And I remember suddenly how sometimes Devlan would stumble over a word when he spoke to me. It was as if something in the language we both spoke had suddenly become foreign and impossible to pronounce. I would cradle the phone against my ear, grinning at the invisible surge of energy from his end to mine.

Once in the car I asked him, 'Is English your first language? Or did you grow up speaking something else?'

He didn't answer. He was staring out of the window. Then he told me a long story about a highly successful lecture he had delivered to universal acclaim the year before.

And I was young. Too young then to have any voices of my own. All I had was two small children and a husband. Devlan was twenty years older than me. He must be an old man now.

I was redecorating the hall the day he first rang me. In my torn jeans, that old shirt of Simon's I've always loved. Paint-splashed. Laura helping me peel the biggest strips near floor-level, little flakes of plaster and paper caught in her hair. 'Oh, look at this bit!' She pulled and a long ribbon of giant flowers came away, trailing from her hand.

'Well done, darling!' I climbed down from the stepladder and bent to examine the state of the wall where she had exposed it. 'But be gentle. We don't want the house falling in on us!'

She looked up at me. I knelt down and picked at a crumb of plaster caught in her fringe. Then the phone rang.

His voice at the other end. Slightly apologetic. 'I hope this isn't an awkward time.'

'No.' I brushed the whitish mess from my thighs. 'Oh, no.'

'Only you weren't at the class last week.'

'No. I'm sorry. I couldn't make it. One of my children was ill.'

There was a pause at the other end of the line. Then he said, 'Have you managed to get access to all the information you need?'

I must have frowned. 'I'm sorry?'

He laughed easily. 'Did you need any help catching up?'

'No,' I said quickly. 'No. I borrowed the notes from Chris Masters. I've got it all, the assignment and everything.'

'Good.' He laughed again. 'And don't worry. We didn't cover all that much ground. Nothing that *you* couldn't find your way round in half an hour.'

Laura was at my knee, tugging at the cloth of my jeans. 'Mummy?'

'I'm not worried,' I said.

A week later he rang again. I was giving the girls their lunch. I left Annie to smear noodles and scrambled egg over the tray of the highchair and got up to answer the phone.

That same voice. 'Is this an inconvenient time to talk?'

'Well, it *is*, rather.'

'Only I just wanted to ask you what you thought about something. I really would value your opinion.'

'Actually, we're just in the middle of lunch.'

'It wasn't really that important. I'd just be very glad to know how the class as a whole was reacting to those ideas we touched on last week. You know. The triangle of needs?' He was smiling. I could hear from his voice that he was smiling.

'Oh, pretty well, I think. As far as I can judge. I can't speak for everyone, of course. But the primary needs seem to be getting ever more urgent and peremptory. I don't think there was too much disagreement about that.'

'And the higher needs?'

9

'Oh, we don't even think about those until all the others are met, isn't that right?'

'You've got it.' He suddenly laughed outright, an infectious laugh. I was laughing too. 'Though I doubt any of the others has grasped it quite as well as you.'

Sometimes he would ring me to talk about the other members of the class. 'That Elspeth Cring seems to have a lot of personal unfinished business,' he would say, or, 'I'm a bit uneasy about Geoffrey. Don't you find him a bit buttoned up?'

'We've all got unfinished business,' I told him. 'We're all buttoned up. It's bloody cold out there.'

I could hear him smiling into the phone.

One afternoon when we got in, the girls both clung to me, pulling on my arms like animals or beggars. Laura was sulking, hanging her head, kicking my shins at intervals with her hard school shoes. Annie was grizzling, her plump face all blotchy. 'What's the matter? Stop it. What do you want?'

I made them two cups of lukewarm cocoa and sat them at the table with a couple of biscuits each. I went back into the kitchen, to where the buggy had fallen over backwards under its load of shopping. I unwound the plastic carrier bags from its curved handles. Bread, eggs, a cauliflower – slowly I began to put the things away. Then I caught sight of the leaf on the counter.

It was a spectacular leaf, deeply serrated, a clear brilliant red. Some kind of ornamental maple. I picked it up and smoothed it against the palm of my hand. I turned it over. Then with my forefinger I traced the veins gently one by one, from where they rose to the tip, and back again, until I had mapped the whole area of its surface. I picked it up by its short stem and twirled it in the late sunlight.

'What are you doing?'

I jumped. 'Nothing.' I turned to look at my daughter, standing there with her cup and that moustache of chocolate across her upper lip. 'What's the matter, Laura? Have you still got room for more?'

Pushing Annie up the hill in the buggy while Laura skipped in front of us, I would stop to pick out the most brilliant leaves from the drift at our feet. Copper beech, burning bush, sumac. Sometimes one would float down to settle on Annie's soft crown and I would detach it gently and give it to her to hold. Laura would arrive at school each morning with a frosted many-coloured fan.

And on wet days they would squelch under our feet, stick to our shoes, clog the wheels. Oak, sycamore, horse chestnut. In some of them the green would drain straight to brown with no transition. I would show Laura how each open hand of chestnut left a tight horseshoe scar on the tree.

The morning the ferry goes down off Sweden I see a leaf hanging from an invisible thread, sunlit, half transparent, green-gold, hanging by its fragile stem and turning. Under black water the bodies must already be surfacing, dragged down by the undertow and slipping up to the dark morning, the bubbles bursting from their lungs like thought and travelling upwards, faster than they can. Or trapped in the long saloons, faces pressed to glass, hands scrabbling at the weatherproof seals, rolled with the currents into a log-jam. The dregs from a cup of coffee bleed into the water, the trays and hand-luggage sliding, and the people following them, catching on the legs of the fixed tables like the ball in a pinball machine. Until it tilts too far and the game is over. As the past lights up their brains with a sound like ringing.

And yet this morning it is so still. The leaf turning and turning like a skater on its invisible surface. When the breeze comes it lifts and dances. But when the breeze subsides it turns perfectly, defining its own perfect surface, creating the thread that holds it, still spinning.

*

Once, about a year afterwards, he rang me. 'How are you?' It was the bland voice.

I was shaking. 'Fine,' I said. 'How are you?'

'Oh, fine.'

'How's business?' I'd heard rumours that he'd set up independently somewhere, offering courses in presentation skills and counselling. Psychotherapy too, I heard. 'How're the power and the authority these days?'

He laughed easily, as if it were a joke we shared.

He must be an old man now.

> *Un gentil amoureux sa nimfe écartant*
> *devient vieil tout à l'instant.*

I am bent over cardboard boxes, checking off the orders, when Oliver calls through to me. 'Jan?'

'Yes?'

He stands behind me in the doorway, his arms dangling. 'Have you heard of a book called *The Unlikely Journey of Mr Fish*?'

'*The Unlikely Journey of Mr Fish*?' I say. 'No. What's the name of the author?'

'I don't know. He doesn't know. And I can't find it on the computer. It doesn't seem to be listed.'

I sigh. 'Try *Books in Print*,' I tell him.

'Okay. Yes.' I hear him go back into the main room of the shop. I hear him mumbling something to a customer, and a low voice answering. I turn back to my boxes. But behind me the dialogue continues. The voices are getting louder. I stand up and brush the dust from my knees.

'Can I be of any help?'

The customer is quite young, in his thirties, probably. He smiles at me, a pleasant open smile, an unruly fringe of very red hair falling forward. Glasses. 'Oh. Yes. Thank you.'

'What did you say the title was?'

'*The Unlikely Journey of Mr Fish*.'

'Are you certain?'

He looks apologetic. 'Well, no. Not absolutely certain. I might have got it wrong. But it was something like that.'

'So if we can just take down all the details . . .'

'Matthew Donaldson.' He looks up at me and half smiles.

'Daytime phone number?' I say.

That afternoon, when the shop is quiet, I ring the number he has given me. An elderly man's voice answers. 'I wonder if I could speak to Mr Donaldson?' I say.

'This is Rex Donaldson speaking.'

'Mr Matthew Donaldson?'

'Oh. Yes. Of course. May I ask who's calling?'

'It's the Castle Bookshop, in the High Street. It was about a book he might have wanted to order.'

'Yes. Certainly. I'll just go and get him.'

There is a long silence, cut with the chink of cups and the sound of a radio. 'Matthew?' I hear him calling. Then there is a clunk as someone lifts the receiver. 'Hello?'

'Is that Matthew Donaldson?'

'Yes.' He sounds breathless.

'It's the Castle Bookshop here. You remember you came in and spoke to some of our staff this morning about a book you might want to order. Well, I've found the title. It's actually *The Impossible Departure of Mr Frisch*. The author's name is Martin Dalucci. You might want to write that down. Then if you do want to order it there shouldn't be any problem.'

'Yes,' he says. 'I've got it. Thank you.'

'So?'

There is another silence.

'So . . . do you want us to go ahead and order it for you?'

'Oh. Yes. Please. If you could.' He sounds embarrassed. He laughs. 'How long will it take to arrive?'

'Oh, shouldn't be too long – a week, a fortnight. We'll let you know when it comes.'

'Thanks.'

'And if you have a change of heart,' I tell him, 'you could let me know.'

'Right,' he says. He sounds puzzled. 'I'm afraid I don't know who you are.'

'Jan Hickman.'

'Okay. Right. I'll let you know. Thanks.'

'It's a pleasure,' I tell him.

When I get home I take off my work clothes and change into jeans, an old sweater with ragged holes at the elbows. I take the make-up off. For a long time I stand looking at myself in the bathroom mirror, trying to see myself through a stranger's eyes.

What was it Wilde said once to an inhibited friend of his? 'The thin lips of someone who doesn't know how to lie'?

My own lips are thin. I pout, trying to push them into a new, fatter, more seductive shape. *Really missing a cuddle.* I push my mouth even further forward, but my lips don't seem to get any plumper. 'Prunes and prisms,' I say. 'Prisms.' And then, 'I love you.' The flesh meets and parts with a little popping sound, like the mouth of a fish.

The next day at almost exactly the same time I ring him again. The same elderly male voice answers. 'Could I speak to Matthew Donaldson?' I say.

Then his voice.

'It's Jan Hickman, from the Castle Bookshop. I'm sorry to bother you.'

'It's no bother.' But he is surprised, I can hear it.

'I just thought you'd like to know that I put in your order last night.'

'Oh? Yes. That was what I understood.'

'Only the title didn't come up on the computer, so it was a little more complicated than usual. We found it, though, eventually. It went into the order book. And we've got your name and phone number, so we can let you know the moment it arrives. I thought you'd like to be kept in the picture.'

'Yes.' He is mystified. I wait for him to put the phone down, but he doesn't. In the end I am the one to break the connection.

And this evening when I get home my lips look perceptibly fatter, the image itself slightly less ludicrous. 'Oh, the triangle of needs,' I tell it. 'Nothing someone like you couldn't find your way round in half an hour.' It grins back at me, its hair sticking out, full of the last of the evening sun, gleaming like a giant bubble. I purse my lips gently and blow.

The next day, at the same time almost precisely, I ring his number again. This time it is a woman's voice, younger than the man's. She sounds harassed. 'Hello? Yes?'

'Good afternoon. This is Jan Hickman from the Castle Bookshop. I wonder if I could possibly speak to Matthew Donaldson?'

'Of course you can.' It's a pleasant voice, in s ite of everything. 'Just a moment.'

When he picks up the receiver I wait for a few seconds. I force myself to count five slowly before speaking. Then I say, 'I'm so sorry. It's Jan Hickman here, of the Castle Bookshop. Have I caught you in the shower, or something?'

He laughs, but he is angry. 'No.'

'It's just that I'm afraid I've got to tell you that the book you've ordered is temporarily out of stock at the suppliers.'

'Oh. Fine. Well, I'm sorry to have troubled you.'

'But it's only temporary,' I say quickly. 'The publishers have assured us that they'll be able to get it to us within another two weeks. So if you'd like to just leave it with us, we'll see what we . . .'

'Fine,' he says. 'That's fine. No hurry.' He bangs the receiver down so loudly that I recoil, my right ear ringing like a shell.

On the last day I wait longer. I wait until almost closing time.

'You can go if you like,' I call to Oliver. 'I'm not in any hurry tonight. I can put the shop to bed on my own.'

Oliver laughs. 'Got some little illicit affair going, have we? Fine. Well, if it gets out of hand, you know where to find me.'

'Shut up, Oliver. Piss off.'

He picks up his jacket and the battered briefcase he uses to carry his sandwiches. He stumbles against a dump-bin of children's books as he goes, sending the bright pictures sliding across the floor. He kneels to pick them up and arranges them haphazardly. Even from here I can see that some of them are upside down. He swings back the door and steps out into the street. I see him stop and grin back at me through the clear glass of the door.

I go out to the little back kitchen and put the kettle on. I make myself a cup of tea with a single teabag. I stir it slowly until it infuses. I sit back in my chair and look at the telephone on its rest just at my right elbow.

For once it is Matthew's voice that answers. 'It's Jan Hickman, from Castle Books,' I say. I savour the words, the sound of my own voice, oddly unfamiliar. I concentrate on keeping my neck-muscles relaxed. It is quite hard not to laugh.

'Yes?' He sounds tense.

'There was just one thing.'

'Yes?'

'When I was going through the order book, late last night, I noticed that we had two copies of *The Impossible Departure of Mr Frisch* on order, both in your name. Were there two? Or was it only one copy you really wanted?'

'Yes. One.'

'Well, that's fine, then. I'm so sorry to have dragged you from your shower, or bed, or evening's entertainment, or whatever.'

'Yes.'

'It's been a hard day.'

'Yes?' He seems to relax.

'So many people badgering you all day long, and yet not one moment of genuinely meaningful human exchange.'

'Yes.'

'Well . . .' The lighter voice now, the laugh. 'Time to cut my losses. It's Saturday. Time to go and find the others at Perry's.'

There is a long silence. I wait for him to break it. I can hear his breathing. 'So . . . Have a good evening,' he says.

I wait then. How long to give it? A month? Three weeks? Even a fortnight seems too long. *They'll come screaming. They'll rave to you about love and death and necessity.* I don't trust it. But two weeks ought to be enough. At five-thirty exactly on the Saturday I push open the door of Perry's wine bar.

The place is almost empty. I order a glass of white wine and sit down at a table by the window, with a good view of the pedestrian crossing. It is a splendid vantage point. I am a private detective. Or God. I look down at the street and recognise the ambling walk and gleaming tonsure of a man I used to know.

I sit drinking the wine slowly. I light a cigarette. Below me young men in macs stride up the hill from the train. A barrier with red and white markings seals off a section of pavement. Little yellow lamps wink on and off. The traffic-light at the crossing goes red and then green again. A slate-blue vehicle drives past almost under me and I look down on its silver top. A woman in a shapeless cardigan leans forward to push a buggy, her face appearing and disappearing with the passing headlights. And then a digger, the great pelican beak folded in front, bouncing as it goes by. I just have time to see the man inside bounce like a doll in his dark seat.

Who or what am I waiting for? I sit at the small marble-topped table, on a wheelback chair, surrounded by green plants. The wooden uprights are festooned with arty decoration – a cluster of bells woven out of twigs, with pine-cone clappers, strings of garlic and onions. And the cross-beams completely hidden under a greying beard of hops.

17

A couple comes in, crosses to the bar. She is short haired, husky voiced, in a black beret. He is half bearded and sandy, a faun in a city suit. They see me watching them and turn their backs.

'You can actually make someone believe they're in love with you,' Devlan said to me once.

I tried to look sceptical. 'Really?'

'Yes. Really. It works every time. I've tried it.'

'Oh yes?' I said again.

'You get them used to seeing you or hearing from you at the same time every day, or every week, or every month, until they get to expect you. You induce a sort of dependency.'

'Wouldn't they just find you predictable and boring?'

'Possibly. At first. But there's the trick. They don't even have to like you. They certainly don't have to harbour any romantic illusions about you. But withdraw the regular dose, and they're hooked. They'll come screaming. They'll rave to you about love and death and necessity.'

'Yes?' I raised my eyebrows.

'Try it. I guarantee it'll bring them running. It works every time.'

I looked at him. His face shone, ruddy with a kind of suppressed excitement. 'Is that what you did with me?'

Devlan laughed. 'Of course not. Do you think someone as intelligent as you could fall for something as simple as that?'

I hear the barman pull a cork. Somewhere a fridge hums. A removal van makes the windows rattle. A British Telecom van stops at the lights, its fluorescent herald blowing a fluorescent trumpet, the body gleaming in passing headlights, split down the centre like a stencil. Two young women cross the road in the wrong place, arm in arm, running, laughing, their sleek hair lifting like wings.

18

'Talk to me,' the song says, 'like lovers do.' I take another long mouthful of wine.

Then I look up and see him standing in the doorway.

CHAPTER 2

FELLAS, FANCY meeting a lady, late 30's, who values love, loyalty and honesty, is slim, intelligent, attractive and slightly insane and lives in rural area.

GENUINE MALE, young 50, good-looking, professional, gsoh, wltm a generous, slim, good-looking lady, 30–35, for fun and good times, possible romance.

DP ROWING MACHINE, adjustable hydraulic action, £25.

SLIGHTLY BOHEMIAN, sensitive, expressive, artistic female, no skeletons, 40, seeks male ditto. Don't get it? Don't answer.

A BEAUTIFUL HEALTHY Ollander plant for indoors, produces lovely pink blooms, 5 foot tall, £8.

SOLVENT, PLACID man, 40, seeks lady over 50, for permanent relationship, no smokers.

For once, we are sitting in Deborah's kitchen, not in my own. It is a Sunday morning. Above us, on a rack, her work clothes are strung up to dry. There is a smell of woodsmoke coming from somewhere, or bonfires. 'Do you ever think of doing something more active?' I ask her.

'What do you mean "active"? Isn't gardening for a living active enough?'

I look across at her hands, hard and still brown in places from the sap of plants, her nails chipped and uneven. 'I didn't mean for a living. I meant in your private life.'

'You think I should buy a mini-trampoline? Then, whenever I saw a man coming down the road, I could leap on to it and bounce up and down and smile at him every time my head appeared over the hedge.'

'Are you good with trampolines?'

'Or I could drive down the road for a couple of miles and pretend I'd broken down. Then I could start pushing the car back up Crobham Hill. You could come with me if you wanted.'

'Seriously,' I say. 'You know you put in one of those advertisements once?'

'The personal column? That wasn't very serious.'

'Have you ever thought of doing it again?'

'Well, no. Yes. Occasionally.' She stands up and begins to sweep some of the rubbish off the table and into the bin. 'Do you mind if I start clearing some of this?'

'Only I'd be glad of the benefit of your experience,' I tell her. 'I thought I might try it.'

'You didn't.'

'Why not?'

'No.' She shakes her head. Her foot releases the pedal-bin with a clang. 'No reason. It might be quite fruitful. There are

23

loads of them these days. They even have what they call a browse-line.'

'That makes us sound like cows,' I say. 'Or book-lovers.'

She looks across at me sharply. 'Have you been reading them?'

'Not yet.'

'Well, there's a paper around here somewhere. I think I just threw it away, in fact.' She rummages in the bin and produces it. It is crumpled and a bit soggy, stained with dark juices in one corner. She spreads it out on the table and starts to turn the pages. 'Here. Here we are. Have a look. Who knows? You might see something. At least you'll begin to get a feeling for the kind of wording that might be likely to get results.'

For ten minutes neither of us says a word. Above us over the doorway the clock ticks. Deborah has turned her back and started to wash up yesterday's dishes. Finally she tips the water away and dries her hands. 'Nothing?'

'Everything,' I say. 'Everyone out there is looking for someone. It's amazing. I never knew I was in such company. Listen.'

Wednesdays are my day off, the day I let Oliver manage on his own. Every Wednesday morning I drive the twelve miles into town to the sports centre, to my aerobics class. Then I go to the supermarket and do my week's shopping. In the evening I read and listen to the radio and write letters. There is no need to think about anything.

The step class is perfect for that. You only have to be part of it for ten minutes and time is something you are in control of. There are only the women's bodies and the music, the sun on the field outside, through angled glass.

Try to keep your eyes on something directly ahead of you. I stand on one leg, my other ankle gripped tight, squashed up against my buttocks. But this morning my balance has deserted me. I sway and hop, my free arm outstretched. Everyone in the room is looking at me and smiling.

*

Matthew and I meet then every week, always at the same time, always at Perry's. The barman gets to know us. 'Hello, again,' he says when I walk in. 'Getting colder. Soon be time to put the clocks back. Winter draws on.'

I smile. 'Dry white wine, please.' Then I change my mind. 'No. Sorry. Make that a Guinness.'

'Half?'

'Pint.'

He raises his eyebrows. 'I see. Like that, is it? But you needn't worry. He's here already.' The garlands drooping over his head are greyer than they were. Some of the fibre bells have lost their clappers.

'Don't give me that, Charlie,' I tell him. 'And your hops need dusting.'

'Tell me about your life,' I ask Matthew. We are walking by the river. It is perfect, a Sunday afternoon. My old camera swings on its cord at my neck. 'You live with your parents, right?'

His boots with their heavy treads make great patterned prints in the soft mud. 'Well, I . . .' he says. 'Yes.'

We walk on a few yards. We squeeze through a kissing-gate and go on in single file. I turn back to look at him. He is bending down, unclipping the dog's lead. The dog bounds away and runs up the path, straight past me, its ears flapping. After a while Matthew catches up with me again. 'It just happened,' he says. 'I'm too old to enjoy living with them, but at the time there was no alternative.'

'You were living somewhere else, before?'

'Yes.'

'With someone else.'

'Yes.'

'And you don't have a job.'

At first he doesn't answer. Then he says, 'I did have a job. But the firm was in trouble. There were a lot of us got made redundant. Last in, first out, you know what it's like.'

'What did you do?'

'Oh . . .' He is embarrassed. 'Does it matter? I was an architect. It was my first job after qualifying. It wasn't ideal. But it was a job. Now . . .'

'Now?'

'Well, now it's the Job Centre every Thursday, and living with my parents. Good as they are. And they *are*!' He looks at me almost defensively. For some reason we have stopped walking. The little dog comes running back to us and stands quivering on its short legs. It shakes its head until the collar rattles. Matthew bends down and strokes its head and it yelps. 'My friend,' he says. 'Stupid animal. What a fucking balls-up!'

There is a long silence. We can hear children's voices shouting and laughing, somewhere on the other side of the river. Closer to us, a blackbird. Then I say slowly, 'What I think I hear you saying is that you feel a complete and utter failure.'

'Yes!' I can't tell whether he is angry, or only stating the truth. 'That's exactly what you do hear me saying!' He turns suddenly on his heels and starts to walk back in the direction we have come. The dog looks puzzled.

'Wait! Matthew! Wait!' I am running after him, slipping and sliding in the black mess of rotting leaves. He stops and turns to look back at me, his hair flaming against a background of leaves and water. I raise the camera to my eye. 'Say "complete and utter failure",' I tell him.

I think about Devlan and what rises is a sickly sweet smell, the smell of shame. 'I think I love you,' I told him once on the phone.

'No, you don't,' he said. 'That isn't what love is.'

'What *is* love?' I asked him.

'It's a deep feeling of mutual esteem and commitment, when two people have been together a long time and know each other well. You hardly know me.'

I had to agree with him. I hardly knew him at all. I didn't

even like him much. But my skin prickled when he was near me. I could hardly bear to stay in the same room with him. I had no vocabulary for what I felt. What could it possibly be but love?

We came out of the restaurant together, and stood blinking at each other in the sunlight. There were people everywhere, around us on the pavement, leaning from upstairs windows, spilling into the street. Someone jostled me and I felt the flow begin to take me. Across the surge of bodies I reached out my hand to him.

He caught it and held it. He was looking down at me and grinning. 'Fucking carnival,' he said.

We were trapped, teetering together on the edge of the kerb, with a press of people behind us. Already the advance guard of police in cars and on motorbikes was sweeping the road for the floats and massed bands. Just opposite us, on the other side of the road, I thought I could see someone I knew.

'Let's get out of here,' I shouted, my words carried away from him on a gust of new noise.

Devlan looked at me and shrugged. 'How do you suggest we do that? I can't move. We'll have to wait until they've gone past.'

Just by my left foot there was a puddle of melting ice-cream, greenish and sticky, a broken bit of wafer floating in it like a fin. Slowly I was being pushed towards it. The soles of my shoes were sticking to the pavement. When the first band came, the mess seemed to shake with the drumbeats, sucking me in.

And then the majorettes.

They had no band. Only a truck with taped music blaring through a loudspeaker, strident and distorted. And the little girls high-stepped in ragged formation, their grubby white plimsolls just out of sync. They were concentrating so hard they had forgotten to smile.

And then the star of the show, an adolescent girl in a shiny

27

purple leotard with spaghetti straps that kept slipping from her plump shoulders. She would have to keep reaching sideways to pull them up. It was like a tic. She advanced on us slowly, scowling, staring down at her feet. Above her the silver baton flashed in the air, spinning at her fingertips. Until she stopped and caught it and reached down for her strap. And then she would begin again. The baton was just a spinning silver haze above her head, throwing back sunlight. And then she dropped it.

It fell just in front of where we stood. We saw it bounce and roll sideways into the gutter, almost at our feet. I could feel the blush rising from my chest to my neck as she bent to retrieve it, the flesh between her straining purple straps pale and bulging. As she fumbled for the silver wand she looked up for a moment and we saw her face. A round hot face with little damp wisps of hair sticking to it at the temples. Our eyes met. I tried to smile. Then I felt myself being steered gently and firmly through an opening in the crowd.

'God!' I said. I could hardly breathe.

The people were thinning out now. We didn't have to shout any more. But Devlan leaned over me slightly. 'What's the matter? Didn't you like it?'

'Did *you*?'

'Oh . . .' He was guiding me away from the car-park, in the direction of the station. 'Actually I thought it was rather artistic,' he said.

And how did it begin, really? With the books? The books he lent me, almost against my will? The books of mine I forced on him afterwards? I can't even remember the titles. I come across them sometimes on shelves and my fingers pass over them, as if they had never existed. They were great books, of course they were – only written about foreign people in foreign countries. They were his favourites.

'Well?' he would ask me as I handed the dog-eared paper-

28

back over. 'What did you think?' It was the young voice. He was looking at me with a kind of eagerness.

'A bit predictable, I thought. Very competent. Some lovely descriptions. But a bit long.'

He laughed. 'I like long books. I like something with a bit of weight to it. Didn't you get a feeling for that whole society, the sheer impossibility of that whole relationship?'

'Oh,' I said. 'Yes, I suppose so. A bit self-indulgent, though, didn't you find?'

'Who? The hero? Or the woman?'

'The writer,' I said.

'Do you think I should change my image?' I ask Deborah one afternoon. We are having coffee in the kitchen of my cottage. Sun streams in across the table, lights up her hands on the mug.

'What do you mean, change your image? Isn't it changing all the time?'

'Not really. I mean . . . Look at you. You change your clothes or your hairstyle about every six months. And here am I, the same as I was ten years ago. The same hair, the same wardrobe.'

'The same obsessions,' she says, and laughs. 'What do you want to do, try to grow a beard, or something?'

'I could get my hair cut,' I say.

'Why would you want to do that?'

I reach behind my neck and pick up the heavy tail of hair that hangs down between my shoulder-blades, tangling as it sticks to my sweater. 'I'm going grey,' I tell her. 'Old women look pathetic with long hair, don't you think?'

She laughs again. 'At least your wrinkles are all in the right places.'

'But don't you think that if I tried I could make myself . . .?'

'Well, I'm only your friend, of course, but I must say I find you quite acceptable. Though the pink flowered DMs do clash just slightly with the orange Lurex . . .'

29

Now I'm laughing with her. The coffee in our cups spills over on to the wood of the table and I don't bother to wipe it up. 'It was just a thought,' I say.

She looks at me shrewdly, suddenly serious. 'What's all this image business in aid of?'

One morning as I crossed the car-park Devlan seemed to come at me from nowhere. He was holding something. 'Here,' he said. 'I thought you'd like to borrow this.'

'What is it?'

'A record.'

He put it in my hand. From the sleeve a group of men in polo-necked sweaters gazed out at me, smiling. They looked apologetic. I turned them face downwards. 'What is it?' I asked again.

'Madrigals. From all over Europe. You'll enjoy them.'

'I'm not sure I ...'

But Devlan was already halfway to the door. 'Give it a try,' he called back over his shoulder. 'You might surprise yourself.'

As soon as I got home I got the record out of my bag and looked at it again. As Annie plastered herself with a mess of shepherd's pie and carrot I sat quite still and tried to listen. I tried playing a single track over and over again until I could repeat the words perfectly, without understanding. I left the same track on while I wiped the tray of the highchair and folded up the plastic sheeting under the legs. I played it to the pop and hiss of the kettle, to the low roar of the vacuum-cleaner. When Annie clung to my knees and grizzled I turned the music up louder.

> *Of all the birds that I do know,*
> *Philip my sparrow hath no peer;*
> *For sit she high or sit she low,*
> *Be she far off, or be she near,*
> *There is no bird so fair, so fine,*

Nor yet so fresh as this of mine;
For when she once hath felt a fit,
Philip will cry still: yet, yet, yet, yet.
For when she once hath felt a fit,
Philip will cry still: yet, yet, yet, yet,
Yet, yet, yet, yet, yet, yet,
Yet, yet, yet, yet.

One night, when I couldn't sleep, I played it quite softly. Our basement kitchen was almost in darkness. As the voices met and parted and met again I could just make out the railings, a battered fern brushing the window. I went to the tap and poured myself a glass of water. I took a sip and felt it go down, tracing a path of cold. And in the sleeping house the voices sounded suddenly like my own voice, chasing itself with clipped echoes.

Punch in front of you, keep your hips still, let your shoulders go with it. Monkey plié, lunge and stretch. DON'T LET THAT RIGHT KNEE ROLL IN.
I am grateful for the Wednesdays. Around and in front of me the women's bodies echo one another, right knees square to the mirror, left legs extended. Eighteen women stare back at me, their right legs straight as felled tree-trunks. They peer up at themselves from under damp hair, unselfconscious, admiring. The past is a line of majorettes reflected in a long mirror. No one breaks the pattern. There is only the present, this heavy bass, a complex sequence of steps, constantly changing. One of us, somewhere near the back, still manages to look like a garden gnome.

And later, as I drive carefully out of the sports centre carpark, negotiating the sharp bends, my elbow just brushes the centre of the wheel. The horn sounds. A woman in front of the bottle-bank looks up, the bottle arrested in mid-air, inches from the hole. She is one of the women from the step class. She smiles at me in recognition. She thinks I have sounded the horn on purpose, to say goodbye. Now she will have a special feeling towards me, there will be a bond between us. If I sound my horn a second time she will lift the bottle higher and wave it at me in greeting as I drive away.

Matthew is sitting at our usual table by the window. I see his hair lit up more brilliantly than usual as a truck passes just underneath. He looks up at me and grins. 'On the hard stuff, are we? Sit down.'

I sit down opposite him and struggle to take off my jacket. 'It's getting cold out there.'

'It's warm in here. Even warmer, now you've come.'

He is laughing at me. But I lean forward to where his hand lies across the table and put mine over it. 'What kind of week have you had?'

'Oh, you know. The same. Rex and Sheila still at my back.'

'What for?'

'Oh . . . You know, the usual.'

'Did the Job Centre come up with anything?'

'What do you think? Car-park attendant, community project at the museum for next summer.'

'*Next summer?* Are they sure you're going to live that long?'

'That's what I told them.'

'And Emma? Any news?'

'There's never any news from Emma.' He drinks the head from his beer. The moustache of froth on his top lip makes him look suddenly ten years older.

'Don't you expect to hear from Emma?'

He takes a long drink, the bottom of the glass tipping towards me, eclipsing his mouth. He wipes the froth off on his sleeve. Then he says, 'I don't expect to hear from Emma, ever.'

'Isn't that rather a pity?' I say.

For a long time we sit there in silence, watching the traffic pass underneath us in the darkness. The roadworks have gone now. There are no little amber lights winking any more. The pavement is free and clear. Then a child walks along it, pushing a doll in a toy buggy. She turns and looks back. Someone is calling her. Then the mother appears, half running, struggling to keep up. She grabs the little girl by the arm and pulls her round roughly. 'Guess what? I've brought you a book,' I say.

'Oh . . .' Matthew leans sideways, reaching into his pocket for a packet of cigarettes and a disposable lighter. Then he thinks better of it and puts them away again. 'I don't get time to read all that much lately.'

'You'll like it,' I tell him. 'This one is different. Trust me.'

'What's it about?'

'Oh . . . That's not very easy to answer. I suppose it's about . . . self-sacrifice.' I laugh at his face. 'The ironies of.'

'I'm not sure I . . .'

I pull the book out of my bag and put it down in front of me. I turn it round to face him and push it over the polished table to his side.

He picks it up, turns it over. He is reading the blurb on the back. 'Look, it's very kind of you and all that, but I really don't think I . . . I'm actually rather more into fantasy.'

'Yes, well, I'm afraid fantasy's something I've never really had much time for. Anyway, try it. You might surprise yourself.'

He shakes his head. 'Look, it's okay, all this, I really enjoy seeing you, and everything. But you don't have to try and change things. Honestly. You don't have to open my mind. It's been opened once, and that's quite enough for anyone. Let's just leave it as it is, shall we?'

I concentrate on my voice. It's something I've been practising for days. 'I only wanted to share it with you, because it's a book that used to mean so much to me, and because you're so . . . Because I felt we were . . .' He doesn't laugh. He doesn't even look at me. 'But if you'd rather not take the risk . . .' I get up and take my glass back to the bar. Then I come back to the table. I pick up my coat and start to put it on.

33

'Where are you going?'

'Home. It's half past six already.'

'But we haven't had time to talk.'

'We can talk next week,' I say. 'If you still want to, of course.' I start to walk towards the door. In the mirror I see him reach into his pocket again for the cigarettes. He takes one out and starts to light it. At the door I turn once to look at him. He isn't looking at me. As I hesitate I see him pick up the book and open it at the first page.

When I get home I say it again, to myself, in front of the mirror. 'I only wanted to share it with you,' I say. 'Because you're so . . .' My voice cracks. 'Because I felt we were . . .' My other self looks back at me, slightly puzzled.

The mirror is dark in one corner, the thin ripple of black along its lower edge swelling into a blister, spreading in a slow rash of rust. 'And because I know you value love, loyalty and honesty.' She raises one smeared eyebrow at me and starts to laugh.

The next week he is there again. 'Hi,' I say. 'How was the book?'

'Fine. I can't say I understood it all.' He hands it back to me, and I put it in my bag. I am surprised to see how dog-eared it is.

'Well, you read it. That's the main thing.'

He doesn't answer. There is a sort of boyish excitement about him, something I can't quite place. Then he says, 'And now I've got something for you.'

'What is it?'

'Music.'

'What kind of music?'

'Guitar music.'

'Rock? Jazz?'

'Classical.'

'I didn't know you were interested in the guitar.'

'Yes. Well. While I was with Emma, I used to play quite a bit. Not so easy these days, with Rex and Sheila breathing down my neck, asking me if I shouldn't be writing job applications. But I did . . . well . . . I did love it. I still do.'

'Is this one of your favourites?'

'Yes. Always has been. Well, I can't begin to play it like that, of course. But I have a good bash. I'd get there, if I had half an ounce of encouragement.'

'I'm looking forward to hearing it.'

'Here . . .' He hands it across to me almost shyly. I see his hand shake.

I take it from him and turn it over. I read the title and the names of composer and artist. Then I hand it back. 'I'm sorry,' I say.

'What's the matter?'

'It's a CD. I'm afraid I don't have the technology.'

'Oh.' He looks crestfallen.

'Perhaps I could get a vague impression of what it's like if you were to play the piece to me one day yourself?'

'Oh . . . I'm not very good. I told you.'

'I don't mind.'

'I'm not sure I've got the heart to play really any more.'

I lean forwards across the table and look into his eyes. They are hazel, the tiny flecks in them like live dust. 'But you *should*,' I tell him. 'However badly. It's so important to release all that tension in some kind of creative activity. For your own mental and spiritual well-being.'

He grins at me then, across the table. He covers my hand with his and closes his fingers tightly. It hurts. 'You cow,' he says. Then he picks up my hand and puts it against his cheek.

What was it? Why did I? One grey morning, when I had taken Laura to school and Annie was bedded down for her rest, I picked up the phone. My fingers slipped in the holes as I dialled his work number. 'James Devlan,' the businesslike voice said.

My hand on the receiver was shaking. I almost hung up. 'You have to stop avoiding me,' I said.

Silence. Then the light bland voice took it up. 'And how do you think the situation might be improved?'

'You have to come. I need you to talk to me. Now.'

'Right.' He had hung up. I blinked as I straightened my back. The kitchen looked as if it had been hit by a small explosion. Piles of the girls' clothes lay tangled on the floor. Every worktop was hidden under a sliding mess of dirty plates. A blue-flowered curtain trailed its hem in a bowl of half-eaten cereal. I turned on the radio and rolled up my sleeves.

Within half an hour he was there, sitting on the other side of my dining-table, a mug of coffee between his hands.

'It must be some kind of love,' I was saying to him. 'I feel so dreadful. I can't go on like this. I can't bear my life.'

He looked down at the surface of the table, where it was nicked and scratched by the girls' toys. 'You're making me feel very uncomfortable,' he said. 'Do you realise how uncomfortable you're making me?'

I put my hands over my eyes. I was starting to shake again. I thought I might be sick.

Then he said, 'Listen. How about this?'

I looked across at him, chewing the inside of my lip.

'Say we start going out together for a while? Once a week or so. A film, or a concert. Go up to town. How would you feel about that?'

I wanted to laugh. 'Okay,' I said. 'Great.'

'Good. I'll come and get you on Friday at about six-thirty. But now . . . I must get back to the office. They'll be screwing something up.'

I went with him to the front door. I wanted to say something grateful and ordinary, anything. But I could hear Annie fussing over my head, the cot creaking as she stood up and rattled the bars. 'Just a minute,' I told him.

When I came down with her in my arms he was standing in the doorway, the front door already open behind him. He bent down to peer into Annie's face, blotched pink with pressure-marks, the weave of the honeycomb blanket printed across one cheek. He raised his hand to touch it. 'Sleepy child,' he said, in the softest voice he had. She looked at him steadily. I watched his hand travel over her, from the soft hair at her crown to the damp flattened curls under her ear, the little downy hollow at the base of her neck.

This morning as I cross the café on my way back to the dance studio, I glance out through the angled glass, down at the diving pool, as I always do. But this morning the surface is striped with wide ribbons of light, ribbons which dance and yet seem not to move, clinging in flakes to the shivering surface, and yet somehow three-dimensional, growing up from the depths of the blue water. I move sideways and they move with me. They are following me towards the door. I can make the empty pool flicker like flame.

And what I feel is joy. I move again and watch it move. I stand still and see the deep light settle to the bottom. When I decide to move again, the little tongues will obey me.

It was dark and cold, an evening in February. We walked up and down Baker Street, shivering, our heads lowered against the wind. 'There used to be a good fish restaurant somewhere around here,' Devlan said.

We trudged another fifty yards and stopped again. We turned round and went back. 'It was a good place,' he said.

'It doesn't matter.'

'What kind of food do you like?'

'Anything. I don't care,' I said. 'I mean, I like everything. You choose.'

'Right,' he said grimly. We were standing in a lit doorway. 'Let's go in here.'

We slid into a booth. Someone put a menu in my hand. I

turned the pages, waiting to see what he would order. 'Cress soup, I think,' he said. 'And the salmon.' He looked across at me and raised his eyebrows.

'Yes,' I said. 'Give me that as well.'

When the soup came it was somehow greyer than I had expected. For a while we ate in silence. I concentrated on not choking or spilling anything as I lifted the spoon to my mouth. The grey-green tide in the wide plate in front of me gradually receded. 'I suppose it's all only a matter of market sensitivity,' a voice said.

I looked up. Over Devlan's shoulder I could see the people in the booth next to ours. They were all men, dressed uniformly in suits and ties, all pink skinned and well fed. One of them was balding slightly. I caught the glint of his scalp. 'Or it could just be *wrong*,' a different voice said.

'Look, let me run it past you again, can I?' I saw Devlan grimace. 'There may be some obvious factor we're overlooking here.'

He reached past me to push open the glass door and I stumbled out into the street. The wind hit me in the face. 'I'm sorry,' Devlan said.

'What about?'

'The indifferent meal. Those people.'

'They were all right,' I said. 'They didn't bother us.'

He hesitated, shivering. 'I suppose that's my world,' he said. 'My language. I'm quite comfortable with all that. And of course it would seem like double Dutch to you.'

He had chosen the film. It was a film about a lesbian relationship. Out of the corner of my eye I was watching him. It was something he had seen already and could recommend, he said.

It was about whispering. When the two women made love their whispers filled the darkness – fragments of words, sentences, endearments, washed over their hands and mouths in a flood of half-audible desire. I let it roll over me. I loved the women, all of them. I wanted the whispers to go on outside in my real life, drowning ordinary speech. Devlan held up my coat. I poked my arms awkwardly into the armholes and lifted my hair free. 'Did you enjoy it?' he asked me.

'What? Oh. Yes.' I started to tell him how generous one of the women was, how her generosity had touched me.

'But she let herself be manipulated, totally. She didn't have any power at all in that relationship!'

'No,' I said. 'But she *felt* something. And that's a kind of power.'

'Don't be disingenuous,' he said.

'Have you thought how much older I am than you?' I ask Matthew.

'How old are you?'

'Forty-three.'

'That's not so old. It's not such a big difference.'

'More than ten years.'

'Not that much more.'

Matthew stares out at the road ahead of us. My fingers on the wheel are quite relaxed. I take it a bit further. 'It's not so much that I'm old,' I say. I take my eyes from the road for a brief moment to smile at him. 'It's that you're young. You haven't had time to have much experience of anything.'

'Like gas-lamps?' he says. 'Like domestic servants? Like trench warfare?'

'You could say that.' We round a sudden bend. I have forgotten to slow down. A small open truck is coming towards us, loaded with timber. I brake hard and swerve. Twigs from the hedge scrape and snap against the side of the car.

'Have you ever been married?'

We are sitting close to each other on a sort of settle, in front of a log fire, at the Grasshopper. Our knees are almost

39

touching. 'Of course I have. I've got two grown-up daughters, didn't I tell you?'

'No.' Matthew looks surprised.

'Well, I have. They've both left now, though. One's doing research, and one's in France. But I do get to see them from time to time.'

'And your husband?'

'Simon? What about him?'

'Where is he?'

'God knows. Disappeared off the face of the earth.'

'What happened?'

The flames dart out to wrap themselves round the logs and then disappear. There is only a lick of black across the bark like a shadow to show where a flame has been. 'He turned into a shirt,' I say.

After that we talk about Simon often. Almost every time we meet. In all our encounters Simon is the invisible third.

'What did he do?' We are in the sitting-room of the cottage, books and magazines strewn on the rug between us, the dregs of a mug of coffee close to Matthew's foot.

I pick it up and take it into the kitchen. I rinse it out under the tap, slowly. When I come back in I say, 'He was a barrister. Rather successful. He was beginning to see he could have anything he wanted.'

There is a silence. I look across at Matthew. He is staring out of the window at the trees on the horizon. A group of Scotch pines, twisted and battered by the prevailing wind, easily recognisable from any direction for miles around. His wrists droop across the folds of his cord trousers. He turns round and looks at me. We look at each other. 'Would you like to see a photograph?' I say.

I go over to the desk and rummage in one of the drawers. I pull out a small passport photo and hand it to him.

He studies it for a long time. 'He's a bit like you, actually,' he says.

'Well, they do say husbands and wives get to be like one another after they've been together for a while.'

'How long was it?'

'Seven years. Classic.'

'Do you think if we stay together for seven years you'll get to look a bit like me?'

I laugh. He raises the photo almost to his face to study it more closely. I can see that there is something written on the back. I lean over and twitch it from his fingers. 'We can go to church in identical sailor outfits.'

'You do know I love you?' he says suddenly.

I almost gasp. I've been waiting for this moment, but still it takes me by surprise. I breathe in, then out slowly. 'You're crazy,' I say. I taste the words. 'Do you know what love is?'

'What is love?'

'It's when two people have known each other a long time and have a feeling of deep mutual commitment and respect. You hardly know me.'

He looks at me, theatrically incredulous. But his eyes are shining. 'I do know you. I don't give a fuck about respect. What's respect? But I do know you. At some level I recognise you. And all . . .' He waves his hand across my familiar furniture. 'This.'

I give him a wry smile. I let my voice shake. 'But let's not call it love,' I tell him. I go to the desk again and slip the photo of my brother back in among the others.

I played the record over and over again, trying to like it, trying to hear what he heard in it. It still seemed outlandish, rebarbative. But eventually I began to get a feeling for one or two of the songs. Men's voices interweaving. Counter-tenors almost as pure as the voices of girls. One track in Italian seemed to be repeating 'Electric chair, electric chair'.

CHAPTER 3

CHRISTIAN MALE, 39, separated, two teenage boys, seeks honest, caring Christian female, 27–37, for companionship. Must be patient.

HEADBOARD, DRALON, PURPLE, 4′ 6″, good condition, £12 ono.

LIBRIAN LADY, early 50's, n/s, seeks solvent younger man to love. Car owner preferred.

GENTLEMAN, 49, 5ft 4, slim build, no ties, moving from North, looking for employment and genuine ladies similar age, shy, long-term relationship.

PETITE FEMALE war baby, gsoh, enjoys eating out, pubs and clubs, travel. House, own transport.

VICTORIAN CLOCK, INLAID marble, walnut or similar, nice grain, temple effect, pillars, £100.

'You choose the film this time,' Devlan said.

My mouth had gone dry. 'I can't choose,' I almost told him. The Sunday papers were full of films I had no interest in seeing. 'There *is* something I'd like to go to,' I said.

We queued endlessly in a loud throng. I imagined myself ducking out of the line and running all the way to the station, pushing through laughing people, panting as I raced away from him towards a waiting train. Then we reached the front. I felt in my bag. But I had run out of the house to meet him, leaving my purse on top of the fridge. 'I'm sorry. I must have forgotten to bring my money.' I shivered at the high, childish sound of my own voice.

He was casual. 'Don't worry. You can owe it to me.'

'Yes,' I said. 'I'm sorry. I'll give it back to you next week. With interest.'

He didn't laugh.

We sat side by side in the full cinema, our faces pointing towards the screen. I craned to see over a woman with big hair. Someone seemed to be falling in love. Then someone died. As I watched, shame rose in my throat with a taste of nausea. In the seat next to mine he appeared to have fallen asleep.

It was about then that the voices started getting out of hand. Devlan would say something to me in one voice, and what I heard was accompanied by another rendering, gentler and subtler. My own voice joined them sometimes, as deep as a man's, as the strain was taken up by a kind of falsetto that set my teeth on edge, cracking on the high notes. And sometimes there would be a whole chorus of voices, interweaving like a madrigal, the silly refrain of fa-la-las repeating itself endlessly in some incomprehensible old European language I seemed to understand.

Sometimes I would pick up the phone and hear nothing but silence. I knew he was out there. Sometimes I would seem to hear a whole chorus of male voices singing.

I leave my car in a street two blocks away from where Matthew lives and walk to his front door. It is an ordinary house, a semi-detached chalet bungalow, built probably in the 1960s. The front lawn is neat, green, free of clover or daisies. A circular bed of heathers and miniature evergreens has been carved out of the centre. For a moment I stand there looking up at the window that must be his, my eyes on the point at the centre where the wooden struts cross. I imagine his head appearing behind them.

I walk up the path and ring the bell. A plump woman in tracksuit pants comes to open it. Over the shapeless trousers she is wearing an apron, but her greying hair is tidy, gathered into a tortoiseshell clip. Sheila. 'Is Matthew in?' I ask her.

She looks taken aback. 'Matthew? Yes. I think so.' From the hall behind her comes the smell of the Sunday roast, stewed fruit, greens. She turns and calls back into the house, 'Rex? Is Matthew up yet?'

She goes back inside, leaving me standing on the doorstep. I hear her bustling about, the sound of low voices. Then Matthew comes down the stairs, still sleepy, his clothes rumpled, the lock of hair falling over his eyes. He has forgotten to put on his glasses. He blinks at me. 'Jan?'

'I brought back the book you lent me.'

'But there wasn't any hurry. You could have kept it. I thought you . . .' He reaches up to scratch his left ear. 'You'd better come in.' Behind him in the shadow of the stairs Sheila is still hovering. She turns away and goes back into the kitchen. We follow her into a light bland room full of steam. Matthew shifts his weight from one foot to the other. 'Here.

Have a chair.' I hear him laugh. It sounds rueful. 'Can I get you a cup of coffee, or something?'

'That would be very nice.'

We sit together at the kitchen table. Behind us his mother is draining potatoes into a colander, arranging them in a roasting tin. I put the book in his hands. 'Good,' I say. 'I couldn't put it down. I had to tell you.'

He buries his face in the mug. He peers at me over the rim. Then he says, 'I'm glad to have found you something you could identify with for once.'

'Oh . . .' I raise my voice slightly so that his mother can hear me. 'I wouldn't say . . .'

The door bursts open and Frodo rushes in on us, yelping, licking Matthew's hands.

'Quiet, you silly dog!' Matthew reaches down and fondles the place behind the long ears. Then he pushes him away.

I pat my knees and Frodo jumps up on to my lap, his chin resting on the edge of the table. 'Crazy dog,' I say. I lift one of the long ears and blow into it gently. Matthew is watching me. I let my hand slide slowly over the long muzzle, down among the deep fur of the neck.

'I've got us tickets for a concert,' I tell Matthew.

He looks at me, warily. 'What kind of concert?'

'It's all right. Don't worry. It's something you'll like. Guitar music. Debussy, Fauré, Granados – duets.'

He seems to relax. Then he remembers. 'But where is it? I'm not sure I can rise to . . .'

'Don't worry,' I tell him again. 'I understand all that. This is my treat.'

On the train we find ourselves in a crowded carriage packed with foreign students. Around us on the floor there is a pile of multi-coloured rucksacks. Matthew moves one of them aside with his foot and stretches out his long legs. 'This is the life!'

I turn to look at the scenery and see only his lit face superimposed on the dark bank. We sit very close together, our thighs touching. I lean into his neck, as if I am going to kiss him, and then move away. He puts his arm round my shoulders and I let it lie there until he begins to feel self-conscious about it. The train enters a tunnel. I feel my ears pop. The rush of darkness drowns out the unintelligible conversations all round us. For a moment I am dizzy. Then I feel him take his arm away.

The seats I have chosen for us are in the front row, almost under the platform. When the rest of the auditorium is in half-darkness, we are still in the light. But Matthew doesn't notice. His face is rapt, watching the performers. I can hear him breathing. When I steal a sideways look at him his flecked irises behind the lenses seem to glisten. Very quietly I let myself sink down into my seat and close my eyes.

We were in a pub, by a log fire, the horse-brasses on the side of the chimney-breast glinting. I was looking down into my drink. 'Devlan?'

'Yes?'

I looked up. 'What did you think of me, at first?' I had to know.

'What did I think . . .?' He hesitated. Then he said, 'What I was first aware of in my dealings with you was a feeling of absolute scorn.'

It took my breath away. The beer round the base of my glass was spreading across the polished table in spidery patterns. 'I'm sorry?' I said.

'Scorn. When you looked at me you seemed totally scornful of everything I represented.'

I began to smile. '*Me?*'

He looked at me.

'You seemed to have everything I hadn't had.'

'*Me?*' I said again. 'What did I have? Are you sure you've got the right person?'

'The linear development. That's what I envied.'

For a long time I didn't answer. I concentrated on keeping my voice steady. When I spoke it was several tones lower than usual. 'And where did the line lead?' I asked him.

'Tell me about Simon,' Matthew says.

' "Tell me about Simon," ' I say, and laugh. 'I've told you about Simon. I'm always telling you about Simon. I've told you all I remember. What else could you possibly want to know?'

He kicks at a loose stone on the pathway and it goes spinning into the undergrowth. Brambles. 'Frodo? Where are you, old friend?' The dog comes trotting out of the bracken, and stands for a moment looking at us. Then it bounds ahead along the path and we follow.

'If I tell you any more I shall have to start inventing it.'

His hands are in his pockets. He flaps the sides of his anorak against his body to keep warm. He is shivering. 'Tell me about you and Simon in bed,' he says.

'He was magnificent. When he had a hard-on I used to fix a torch to it with a rubber band to warn the local aviation.'

Matthew smiles. But his teeth are chattering. 'Seriously.'

'Seriously . . .' I pretend to consider. Then I say quietly, 'What do you want to know?'

'Well . . .' He has stopped the absurd flapping now. He is standing quite still. We are facing each other across the path. 'Did he give you . . . satisfaction?'

'Did I give him satisfaction, you mean? No, I shouldn't think so. I tried to. But I don't think I did. Does one ever?'

'Did he?' Matthew says again quietly.

For a long time I don't answer. The network of little paths twists away from us in all directions like the legs of a giant spider. Above us a few dry leaves are still clinging, rattling in the wind. 'I cared about him. I really did. And I think he cared about me.'

'But sex?'

49

'Oh, sex,' I say. 'Yes. Like a drug. Like going back into the womb. Like dying. For him, I don't know. I won't ever know.'

'*Like dying*? Have you actually ever seen anyone die?'

'I've *heard* someone die.'

'When?'

'When I was twelve. I was in hospital to have my tonsils out. An old woman died in the night in the next bed. I heard her. She was gasping for breath for what seemed like hours. Sort of rasping. And then the rasping stopped. It was at Christmas,' I add, irrelevantly.

Matthew is perceptibly paler. He picks up a twig and throws it at the water. It falls short and lands on the bank, in a clump of reeds. 'Don't worry about it,' I tell him. 'And you did ask.'

Before the week was up he rang me. 'I don't think we arranged where we were going to meet.' It might have been some business arrangement.

'I'm sorry. I was half assuming you'd pick me up.'

'I will pick you up,' Devlan said quickly. 'Of course. Only you might prefer me to pick you up somewhere else – at the top of your road, say.'

'But why . . .?'

'It might be more discreet.'

'Oh,' I said. 'Yes. Of course. Fine.' The kitchen was beginning to turn on its axis, the rusty fridge, the bucket of nappies. I closed my eyes. 'Whatever you think is appropriate.'

'By the church, then? Half past six?'

'All right.'

'Friday.'

'Friday.' I hung up the phone and went back to the nappies. I plunged my arms in up to the elbow. Above me I could hear Annie beginning to stir in her cot. Through the party-wall, the sound of a dog barking in a kind of frenzy. Then a man's voice. 'Shurrup, you bugger!' And a dull thud that could have been a kick.

*

At first when I met Devlan at the church he was on time. As I came up the hill I could see his car parked off to one side, under a tree. The next week it was in the same place.

But the week after that he was doing a U-turn at the top of the road just as I arrived. Then the waiting began.

I would shelter in the church porch or sit on the steps at the back. Sometimes the great windows were lit from inside and flakes of red and purple fell across the grass. Sometimes I could hear singing. Once he was so late I let myself slip down in the deep shadow behind a buttress and crouched there with my back against the wall, looking up at the stars.

How many times did Devlan and I sit talking in his car in the dark street outside my house? Three? Four? Not many. Not enough to constitute a habit, or even a relationship. Once when we said goodbye I couldn't get out of the car. 'I'm sorry. I can't do it,' I said to him.

He didn't laugh or tell me to pull myself together.

'I'm sorry,' I said again. 'I just can't leave you *here, now, like this.*'

'What do you want me to do?'

'Drive back into the centre of town. Let me out at the traffic-lights.'

He drove round the block and then back the way we had come.

'Let me out here,' I said. 'I'll walk. I'll feel okay, walking.'

'I'll walk back with you.'

'No. I'm perfectly all right on my own. I'd rather be on my own. Honestly.'

But he parked the car on the hill and walked back with me in silence. My legs seemed to move normally. We walked fast, our shadows growing as we passed under each streetlight, then superseded. At my door we barely said goodnight.

Deborah steps over the threshold into my sitting-room. It's Sunday morning. 'Here,' she says. 'I brought you these.'

'What for?'

'For you. To . . . Well, because you seemed a bit . . .'

'Perhaps I am a bit . . .'

'Oh, for Christ's sake, they're only from the garden! And some of them aren't even from the garden.'

I raise my eyebrows.

'It's just a hobby, like poetry or cake-decoration. I just like going for walks, especially after dark. And I always take a small pair of scissors with me.'

'I'll put them in water.'

I start to go to the kitchen door. I open it and go through. Then, just as I am about to turn on the tap, I hear Deborah shriek. 'What's that?'

'What?'

'Here. On the mantelpiece.'

'It's a clock. Can't you see it's a clock?'

'But it's hideous! Where did it come from?'

I come back in, the vase of water in my hand. 'Yes, isn't it?' Together we stand side by side and look at it admiringly. 'It's my most recent acquisition.'

'But where did it come from?'

'From the newspaper. Where else?'

'You mean you actually . . .?'

'I saw the advertisement, and I just couldn't resist it. The description was so graphic – well, as graphic as you *can* be in a small ad. It's an art form, you know, advertising.'

'What did it say?'

' "Clock," it said.'

'Is that all?'

' "Victorian clock, inlaid marble, walnut or similar, nice grain, temple effect, pillars." '

'How much did you pay for it?'

'I can't remember.'

'You'll regret it.'

'I regret it already. That's what I bought it for. I thought I

52

might as well try to fill my life with things to regret, and achieve a sort of unity.'

She takes the vase out of my hand and starts stuffing the flowers into it. 'These are really fresh. You'll see. They should last a week. I only picked them about three o'clock this morning.'

At the aerobics class I try to make my movements as precise as possible. Four beats forwards. Four beats back. Right arm out, left arm out. I watch myself in the mirror, a small automaton with the hair scraped back from its forehead and a self-consciously stern expression.

But when I go marching forward for the third and fourth beats, the others have already started to march back. The woman in front of me sticks out her left arm almost in my eye. She turns and exclaims in Spanish, her dark eyebrows meeting. I look uncomprehending and stand my ground.

Then it happens again. One, two, *three*, *four*, I count, still moving forwards. And this time it is the middle finger of my right hand that almost catches her on the shoulder. She turns towards me and wraps her arm round my head in a mock wrestling hold, growling something with a lot of rolled r's. She pretends to shake me. When she drops me I move over to stand behind someone else. Now I can't see myself in the mirror any more, only the oblique glass of the window, suspended over grey fields and bare branches, misted with sweat and breath.

This morning it seems they have finished remodelling the women's toilets next to the dance studio. Before the aerobics class I make my way across the cafeteria towards the Portaloos as usual. I press the bar of the heavy glass door.

An alarm goes off. I let go, and the door swings back on its axis. The alarm stops. 'Alarmed door,' the notice says. I try again. The woman behind the counter is calling something to me. On the other side of the glass the Portaloo door stands open, showing the empty cubicles. I lean my weight against the bar again and the sound of the alarm rises all round me, drowning the conversation in the café, filling the whole building.

He lent me his records – *Kát'a Kabanová, Death and the Maiden*, madrigals. I ill-treated them, trying not to listen. Once the tube of the vacuum-cleaner caught under the shelf where the turntable was and made the needle jump, gouging a hole that was easily visible to the naked eye. After that, every time I played it, there was a loud crack, then a few phrases missing, then a repetitive click that accompanied the tripping syncopations of the maiden almost until the end.

I lent him a book I liked. It was a book of poetry. 'No, really . . .' He tried to push my book away. 'I don't get any time these days for reading.'
    'But I've been reading all your books,' I said.
    He took it, grudgingly.
    The next time we met he had it in his hand. He gave it back to me, slipping it into my fingers quickly as we stood in the crowded corridor.
    'Did you like it?' I asked him.
    'Oh. Yes. Of course I did.'
    'I'm glad. It's something I've loved since I was quite young. It's very close to me.'
    He smiled, hesitating. Then he said, 'And it's only fifty pages long. It was so refreshing to read something like that, something you could whip through in half an hour.'

When I let myself into the cottage this evening, the front room seems dark. The windows are too small. The old walls are too thick. A patch of late sunlight falls on the carpet, but as I watch it fades, slides sideways until there is only the thinnest strip of colour, hardly big enough to take my two feet. I stand there watching as one by one the eyelets of my shoes disappear into shadow. I stand there until it gets dark. Then

I curl up on the sofa with Simon's old shirt drawn up under my chin. The soft fabric is warm against my cheek, smelling of my own skin. I roll it into a hard ball and wedge it in tightly, under my jaw. One escaping cuff still tickles my nose and I sneeze. Simon. Does it still smell faintly of him? I fall into a doze. When I wake up I am cold and stiff. I have been dreaming of Matthew. The shirt is damp with sweat. Or perhaps I have been dribbling. I sit up and twist it into a rope. Matthew. His face, his flecked eyes, his grin. I twist the fabric so tightly I hear the threads crack.

One evening at Perry's I say to him, 'Would you like to come back with me, to the cottage?'

'For coffee? To look at your etchings?'

'For a meal. I could whip us up a curry, and a nice salad. And there's some classy ice-cream in the freezer.'

'Tonight, you mean? Now?'

'Yes. Why not? You could ring through to Rex and Sheila, tell them not to wait up.'

'Piss off,' Matthew says.

'Well, couldn't you?' I raise my glass and drain it.

He picks up his own glass and pours half the contents into mine.

'Well, that was a lovely meal.' Matthew looks up at me, his face orange in the glow from the stove.

'Don't mention it.'

'Do I get coffee?'

'Of course you do.'

'And etchings?'

'No etchings.'

'I want to go to bed with you.'

'Of course you do.'

He turns to look at me. 'Don't you want to?'

'No.' I bite my lip. 'Of course I don't.'

*

Almost every night now I take the shirt to bed with me. Sometimes I wear it, over or under my own clothes. Sometimes I sit in the dark and light candles, so that the white of the shirt shines out against a background of shadows. Once as I strike a match the head flies off and hits me on the stomach, burning a small hole. Now the smell is not just my own sweat laced with the faintest memory of Simon – there is the slight but unmistakably acrid smell of burning.

We are in bed together. The light from the village's one street-lamp shines gold through the gap in the curtains. He is asleep, his glasses are folded on themselves on my bedside table. The lenses gleam at me from beside the clock, speckled with something that could be ash.

Gently I pull back the covers. Then I run my tongue slowly from the hollow under his ear to his shoulder, from his shoulder to his navel, from his navel to the fiery bush underneath. He stirs under me. 'Again?' he says. 'Wasn't it any good, the first time?'

'It was interesting.' My mouth is full of hair. 'You might just be able to improve on it, if you really gave it everything you've got.'

And we try it a second time. Then we lie back against the pillows. 'Any better?' he says. He reaches across me for his cigarettes. He lights one. I watch the smoke coil to the ceiling.

'Much better,' I tell him. 'Wonderful.'

'*Like dying?*'

'Like dying.'

He sits up suddenly, the bedclothes falling from his shoulders. He is so beautiful. 'Liar!' He shouts at me. 'Liar! Liar! Liar!' He gets out of bed and stands there naked, the sheets and blankets tangled at his feet. He moves forward as if to grab me by the shoulders and shake me and the bedside table rocks on its base. The lamp slides to the floor with a crash of breaking china. The room has gone dark.

I can feel myself starting to smile. 'What drama!' I say. 'Your

56

poor parents! What a lot they must have to put up with! I don't know how they stand it.'

The next time it is the same. And the time after that. Sometimes Matthew turns over and falls asleep. More often he sits up and smokes a cigarette, staring out of the window at the grey fields. On their distant crest the Scotch pines wave, swaying slightly, their tuft of dark growth bevelled by the prevailing wind.

I sit up and put my hand against his bare shoulder. 'Look, you don't have to . . .' I kneel up against him and rub my cheek on the back of his warm neck. 'It doesn't have to be . . . Not every time, anyway.'

He gets up and starts to pull on his clothes. Underpants, jeans. He buckles his belt. 'Aren't you contradicting yourself?'

I lie back against the pillows, my hands clasped under my head. 'Don't you want me to contradict myself?'

His shirt and sweater are lying on the floor where he took them off, the sleeves of the shirt still inside the sweater like a lining. He pulls them on as if they were one garment. 'Oh, feel free. Be my guest. Change your mind as often as you like. It's just so stereotypically *female*, that's all.'

In spite of myself I sit up and pull the quilt up to my chin. 'Stereotypically female? Are you sure?'

Devlan drove me the long way home, out through the suburbs that linked our two towns. I found myself looking at his profile for clues. On either side of the dark road the trees stretched up into starlight.

Then the trunks thinned and gave on to a jumble of low buildings I recognised. 'That's where Laura and Annie were born,' I said to him.

He glanced across at me in the darkness. 'What was that like?'

'Laura? Or Annie?'

'Laura.'

'Oh . . . Not good.' I shivered. Another couple of minutes and his car slowed to a stop outside my house. 'Not good,' I said again. 'A twenty-four-hour job.'

He switched off the engine and the headlights and turned towards me, his face striped black with shadow. 'And Annie?' he said.

I smiled as I remembered. 'They told me I'd never have a child naturally. I was booked to go for a check-up a month before, to fix the date of the Caesarean.'

'And what happened?' Devlan said quietly. We were holding hands. I could feel the inside of his palm, warm and dry when I moved mine. One by one, I explored the spaces between his fingers.

'I didn't make it as far as the appointment. Annie decided it for herself. She came the day before I was due to go in, in three hours.'

He didn't say anything. For a long time we sat looking out at the road, at the street-lamps with their multiple shadows, the sharp corners of the houses. Then gently he took his hand away.

I unlocked the front door quietly and let myself into the house. The sitting-room was empty, but the television was still on. There was a mug on the floor, beside the armchair, half full of cold coffee, the milk clotted in the centre like phlegm.

The TV screen still flashed out the late-night news, first in blue, then in a reddish glow that lit up the corners of the room. There had been a multiple pile-up somewhere up north, in fog, on the M6. The camera scanned the line of crushed vehicles from above, some of them skewed at odd angles, the bonnets forced open like blackened mouths. Here and there the lights of the ambulances still flashed. A blanket was a streak of crimson. I turned it off. I bent to pick up Simon's pullover, where it lay crumpled on the carpet. A pen fell out of it and rolled across the floor, coming to rest against my knee. Then I stood up.

My underwear was sticking to me. I was wet. And some-thing like desire was pulsing, that familiar ache low down. I leaned against the wall and closed my eyes.

> The silver swan, who living had no note,
> When death approached unlocked her silent throat;
> Leaning her breast against the reedy shore,
> Thus sung her first and last, and sung no more:
> Farewell all joys, O death come close mine eyes;
> More geese than swans now live, more fools than wise.

CHAPTER 4

TABLE LAMPS, DATE uncertain, onyx, swan motif, watered silk shades, £25 pair.

RED HUNKY sweatshirt, were you in Perry Street Wednesday 13th? My van fell in love with your car. Any chance?

MAGIC MALE, 32, dry soh, slim, intelligent, into fantasy and SF, wltm enchanting fag-free fairy for powerful spell.

BENEVOLENT VICTORIAN squire, 30, no other assets, seeks good-hearted wench, possibly for squiress.

ROCKING CHAIR, PAINTED wood, in bits, buyer collects, £5.

BOX LARGE PRINT novels, thrillers, etc., suit elderly person with failing eyesight, £7 the lot.

DUNG GRAB, £650.

We walk by the river often. It is our favourite place. Sometimes we take Frodo with us. More often now we go on our own. One Sunday afternoon in late October the weather is unseasonable. The sun slants through branches, where they lean to touch the surface of the water. Some of the leaves are still green, but in the sunlight they look gold, seeming to move with the reflections. Just under them the current swirls. We stop and sit on the bank. Across the water the opposite bank is already in shadow. 'This is where Simon died,' I tell Matthew.

It is a shock. He turns to face me. 'What did he die of?'

'Oh . . . Grief. Frustration.' Matthew doesn't answer. I look at him. The sun in his hair is dazzling. For a fraction of a second his face is almost unrecognisable. I screw up my eyes. 'Frustration. Or grief. Isn't that all anyone ever dies of?'

For several years the most important person in my life was Bethan. When Devlan and I first met she was seventeen. He would talk about her, her interests and achievements, about the school she went to. At times it reminded me of my own old school. Some of the teachers she had sounded a bit like teachers who had taught me. Their little idiosyncrasies of speech and gesture came back to me as Devlan talked. Sometimes the fear came back with the voices.

'How's Bethan?' I would ask him, and he would seem to tell me the story of my own life.

Once he was angry. At a sixth-form parents' evening the deputy headmistress had said to him, 'She's not one of the high-fliers, you know, your daughter. She's not in the top ten.'

I winced. I could still hear the kind of voice that said something like that, the flat vowels we had had to learn to interpret. 'And what did you say to her?'

'I asked her who she thought she was talking to,' he said. 'I told her my daughter can do anything she fucking well chooses.'

'What does Bethan look like?' I asked him. 'Have you got a photograph?'

He shook his head. The bland voice answered me. 'I don't carry pictures of anyone. I'm sorry.'

'Is she dark? Fair?'

'Fair.'

'Tall?'

'Average.'

The road sped under us, his car eating up the white dashes and throwing them out behind. On either side the flat fields stretched away, silvered in places with a sheen of lying water.

'Taller than me, then,' I said.

'Yes.'

'Fairer than me.'

'Yes.'

'Cleverer than me.'

I wanted him to turn and look at me and laugh. I would have laughed, in his shoes. But he looked grim, his skin reflecting the colour of the road. He flicked on the indicator and changed down. 'Yes,' he said finally. 'I hope she will be cleverer than you.'

One day in the local paper I came across her, in a school netball team, posing in a white Aertex blouse and a crested sweater. She had her eyes shut. I looked for traces of likeness, but there was nothing I could put my finger on. Perhaps she took after someone I had no way of imagining.

'There was something someone said, just before I dropped out of university,' I tell Matthew. 'Something that probably originated in some philosophy class and then got passed around from mouth to mouth, until it got distorted almost beyond recognition, like a game of Chinese whispers.' I pause for breath.

'Go on.'

'Well, I can't remember it exactly, but it was something to the effect that you never actually *have* to put up with your life. You do always have the option of killing yourself. If living really is worse than the alternative, then the logical thing is to choose that alternative. And that logic is always in your possession. You're never totally powerless.'

'That's not always true.'

'No. But almost always.'

'It's not a very cheerful thought.'

'Well, this may sound strange, but actually I always found it a very comforting thought – something I carried about in my pocket for years, a kind of talisman, almost, or a coin in a foreign currency. Like one of those Scandinavian ones with holes in the middle.'

'Or a key,' Matthew says. I look round at him. But his face is turned away from me. He is watching something float past us on the current. It might be a dog, or a lump of wood. 'And this talisman. Have you still got it, now?'

I take something out of my pocket. It glints in the sunlight. Then I close my fingers over it. 'I think it's just about time I got rid of it.' I brace my whole body and throw it, as far out as I can, into the middle of the stream.

'Risk?' Devlan said. 'What do you know about risk?'

'I used to take risks. When I tried to write stories.'

'Rubbish. What's at stake? In the worst possible scenario, what would you have to suffer? *Embarrassment?*'

'Demoralisation,' I said. 'Frustration. Grief.'

'But those aren't real risks. Real risks involve something tangible – money, or goods and services, people's lives. Those are the risks I take every day of my life. You don't know you're born.'

I could hardly speak. 'Don't you think even the intangible things can rebound on you in quite tangible ways?'

'No. Not unless you're fool enough to let them. It's about control.'

'But the truth isn't always controllable. And too much truth can be devastating.'

'How, devastating? Aren't you just being melodramatic, or naïve?'

'Am I?'

'I think so.'

'Well, then,' I said. 'That's it, then. You're quite right. I don't know I'm born.'

Had I asked him, or did he volunteer it? 'There was one who rang me once at two in the morning. Said it was life or death.'

I smiled.

'She said she was going to kill herself as soon as it got light. She wanted me to spend that time with her.'

'Yes?'

'She had the sleeping-pills all lined up ready on the bedside table, in little rows.'

'And did she take them?' I wanted to laugh.

'No. I talked her out of it.'

'And then you went home.'

'No. We ended up going to bed together.'

'And that took her mind off things.'

He seemed not to hear me. I was aware of his breathing. 'She was the one who kept her socks on,' he said.

One night I dream that Devlan has served me with a writ for libel. The strange document is written in green. I turn it over and see his sprawling handwriting. Three stories are implicated. The most damaging of all is something called 'Greensleeves'.

And even the shirt is not the same now. I clutch it to my face and breathe in the warmth of Simon's remembered body and my own, and something burnt. A soft fold of fabric tickles my cheek. But the black smell still rises, dominating the others. I stand up and go into the kitchen. I rummage in the drawer by the sink for the big orange scissors. Then I hack at the blackened edges of the hole until there is nothing left.

'I'm so glad you could come to supper,' I tell Deborah. 'I hope you've got your boots.'

'*Boots?*'

'Wellington boots. Didn't I tell you?'

'They're in the back of the car. That's where I always leave them. Why? What didn't you tell me?'

'I thought we'd go out.'

'Go out to dinner?'

'No. Go out to buy something.'

'A heavy-duty galvanised watering-can, you mean? Or a set of moulds for making garden gnomes?'

I pick up her boots and put them in the back of the Mini.

'Not a piano?'

'A rocking-chair,' I tell her firmly.

We drive along the country lanes, singing. Songs about old men mostly – 'Grandad', and 'When I'm Sixty-four'. Finally I draw up at a farm gate. A track curves round gently towards the door, brown with a residue of slurry. 'I just thought of something,' Deborah says.

'What?'

'How the hell do you think you're going to get a rocking-chair in the back of a Mini?'

'It's all right,' I tell her. 'It's in bits.'

We stumble into the front room of the cottage, the black plastic dustbin-liner dragged between us, knocking against our shins. 'Careful,' I say. Together we lay it gently on the floor. Then we grip the two bottom corners and raise them slowly until the contents slide out on to the rug.

We stare at the pieces. 'There's so much of it!' Deborah's

voice is not much more than a whisper. 'Are you sure this is just one chair?'

'That's what the ad said it was.'

The dowels lie all around us, in a variety of shapes and sizes. Some of them must belong to the back. Some of them must be meant to support the arms. There seem to be more than four legs. There is a flattish piece with a cut-out heart in the middle of it, and a seat with contours for imaginary buttocks. There is a curved piece that must be some sort of decoration. And a single rocker, its dark-blue paint nicked and scratched by a long succession of pumping feet.

For several minutes we stand looking at the pieces. Deborah shakes her head slowly. Then we get down on our hands and knees.

When Deborah leaves there is a full moon. As I open the front door to see her go, I shiver. The white cold light falls on the bars of the front gate, the roofs of the farm buildings opposite. It tangles in branches above my head. 'Drive safely,' I call to her as she turns her key in the ignition. Her car disappears between the high hedges, a last glint of silver.

When I go inside, the rocking-chair is still standing in the middle of the carpet. It seems to be all complete. But something is wrong with it. I stand looking at it, trying to decide what it is. Is one side of the seat higher than the other? Does the back lean out more on one side? Every empty hole has been filled with a wooden rod. Between the two of us we have finally managed to use up all the pieces. There doesn't appear to be anything missing. And yet somehow it still looks slightly odd. Like an exercise in perspective with two different eye-levels, or more than the required number of vanishing-points. I put my hand up to the light switch and turn it off. Then I step forward into the middle of the room and sit down.

It is all right at first. The chair only creaks slightly, as rocking-chairs are supposed to creak. I lean back and look out over white fields. By now Deborah will almost have reached home. She is screwing up her eyes, cursing those last few miles, cursing the oncoming cars that force her to dip her headlights. She looks so tired.

I start to rock. Backwards and forwards, harder and harder, in a kind of dream. And it is then that the first dowel springs from its place with a clatter and rolls across the rug at my feet.

'Linear development' was a phrase Devlan seemed to like. If I had been combing his conversation for buzz-words, 'linear' and 'development' would have been two of them. Yet he seemed intent on telling me my life was moving in small circles.

'If you take a group of people,' he said, 'any representative group of people, and look at what they're doing now, then look at them again in ten years, you find that almost all of them are doing almost exactly what they were ten years before. All the statistics support it. The chances are that in ten years' time you'll be acting and thinking almost exactly as you are now.'

'Have you been doing this for ten years?' I asked him.

He smiled. He looked tired. 'What do you think? Of course I haven't!'

'But I will be?'

'All the statistics . . .'

I cut him off. 'I wouldn't count on it,' I told him.

He shrugged. 'Come and talk to me in ten years,' he said.

> *Or depuis que mon heur nous a rassemblé,*
> *D'un grand aise je suis toujours comblé;*
> *Tout content*
> *Et jamais dolent.*
>
> *Un gentil amoureux sa nimfe écartant*
> *Devient vieil tout à l'instant.*

*

This time we aren't walking by the river. We have turned the other way, through the village and out along a footpath across the fields, towards the Scotch pines. We stop and lean on a gate. From a mile or so away the trees greet us, larger now, the individual shapes of the twisted trunks clearly visible. Matthew gets out his handkerchief and blows his nose. 'How did Simon really die?' he asks me.

The ground at our feet is soft and muddy, trodden into a complicated pattern of superimposed footprints. I lift one foot and bang it on the bottom bar of the gate to knock off the mud. 'It was an aneurysm. It was very sudden. We all of us felt we ought to have known there was something wrong. But we didn't. There wasn't any sign of anything. One day he was just there, and the next day they were rushing him to the hospital. And the day after that we were on our own.'

He seems to stare at the trees. 'That must have been incredibly hard.'

'It was.' I cough. 'And it doesn't get any easier.' I pull myself up on the gate and sit on it, looking over his shoulder, back along the way we have come. He pulls my head down to his and kisses me, licking my face like a puppy. I almost lose my balance. I scream and push him away.

'He didn't kill himself, then?'

'Simon? No, of course not. Whatever made you think he did?'

'Oh, I don't know. Just an impression I had.' He looks at me and I start to laugh. I fall forward and jump free, into a soft squelch of dark cow-trodden earth.

Then we are both laughing. Our laughter echoes across the fields like the laughter of two madmen. It must be audible for miles, from the trees. We gasp for breath. The ache in my side is so bad I can hardly stand.

Two young women are trapped on a mountain, somewhere in Scotland. I hear it on the six o'clock news, one night as I am unpacking the groceries. I stop what I am doing for a

70

moment and straighten my back. It is hard to breathe. Then I finish putting the vegetables away. I cut up onions and fry them in a pan. I add tomatoes and lentils. The bubbles rise to the surface with a small pop, making craters like the surface of the moon. But momentary. I grab a packet of spaghetti and let a small bundle of it slide out into my hand, the delicate filaments pricking my palm. Then I go to the phone and dial Deborah's number. 'Did you hear about those two young climbers?' I say.

'What two young climbers?'

'Stuck on Ben Nevis or somewhere. They haven't found them. The weather's supposed to be atrocious. They've had to call off the search.'

'But they'll start looking again in the morning?'

'Oh. Yes. Yes, I suppose they will.'

'Look, Jan . . .'

'Yes?'

'Stop it.'

'What? Stop what?'

'I don't know. All this. You can't . . .' Her voice is gentle, concerned. 'Are you . . .?'

I can hear myself breathing. 'No,' I say. 'I'm not. I'm perfectly okay. It's just that they . . . I don't know if they'll find them. They say they're seriously worried. You know what that means.'

'No,' she says firmly. 'I don't know what that means. And neither do you. Go to bed early. Get some sleep. They're trained, aren't they? They're not completely stupid. They only have to have the sense to dig themselves in. People have survived for ages in conditions that seemed completely hopeless.'

'How long?'

'What?'

'How long have they survived?'

She coughs. 'Well, I don't know. Ages. Days. Weeks, even. You'll see.'

'Yes,' I say. 'We'll both see. I'm sorry. I'll ring you from work tomorrow. We'll see. We all will.'

'We should try to see less of each other.' We are in bed, Matthew's pale body stretched the length of mine, and beyond.

He looks hurt. 'Why?'

'Because this isn't . . . Oh, I don't know. Can't you feel it? We're poles apart.'

He gets up and starts to put on his clothes, his underpants, jeans, belt. His feet on the floorboards are still bare. 'You're so inconsistent. Sometimes it's as if you've got some sinister hidden agenda. What do you *want*?' He sits down on the edge of the bed. It sinks under his weight. I reach out and stroke his bare side and he catches my hand and holds it away from his body. 'Sometimes this almost reminds me of a TV play I saw once.'

'Yes?'

'About this couple who carried on a relationship over a whole lifetime. They would meet up about every five years.'

'Was it a good play?'

'No. It was crap.' I watch him pull on his shirt and sweater, the shirt-sleeves still tangled inside the sleeves of the sweater, where he took them off as a single garment.

'I'm sometimes quite glad I haven't got a television,' I say.

'What does "gsoh" mean?' Deborah's eyebrows are drawn together in a frown.

'I think it's "good sense of humour",' I tell her. 'I'm not a hundred per cent sure.'

She nods. 'I should think that might come in handy with some of these.' She crumples the newspaper into a ball and aims it at the waste-paper basket.

'What did you think it meant?'

'I don't know. I thought it might mean "good state of health".'

'Perhaps it's the same thing.'

She shrugs. We are eating corn chips and some greenish mess she has made. I can hear her crunching. She leans across to dip a brittle triangle into the green.

'You're not supposed to dip it in twice,' I tell her.

'Why not?'

'Because you give all your germs to the people you're sharing with.'

She turns to stare at me. She looks puzzled. She looks tired. 'But we're not sharing it with anyone,' she says.

When I get to the shop Oliver is already there. The door is unlocked. The lights are on. I go into the back room to take off my coat. Oliver is in the kitchen, standing by the kettle, waiting for it to boil. He looks up when I come in, and grins. 'You know, you ought to get an answering machine,' he says.

'An answering machine? What for?'

'Well, I stayed an hour after you left last night, to put the new books out, and do you know how many phone-calls there were after you'd gone?'

'No. How many?'

'Six.'

'But we were closed. They must have known we were closed.'

'But we're the only bookshop for miles. They still try to get us. If there hadn't been anyone here they would have been forced to try somewhere else.'

'I suppose they would.'

'Actually, it was a customer that suggested it to me.'

'A male customer, or a woman?'

Oliver grins at me again as he hands me a mug of coffee. 'Does it matter?'

Three days later the answerphone is installed. I practise my message, in a variety of different voices. The light young voice. 'I'm sorry. There isn't anyone here at the moment to take your call, but if you would like to leave a message . . .' The bland, colourless voice. The voice that is two tones lower.

But two days later Oliver greets me at the door. 'The machine's dead.'

'What? The computer? Has it gone down *again*?'

'No. Not the computer. The answerphone. The light's not on. The tape seems to have moved forward, but the phone's not working.'

'Shit. Are you sure?'

'Come and see.'

I follow him into the back room. The little light on the answering machine is usually flashing. This morning it isn't even illuminated. 'Well, I'd better get the telephone people out.'

The wire has been cut, just outside the window. The man holds it up for me to see. 'Vandals,' he says. 'You wouldn't think it would happen, in a small place like this, but these days . . .'

'Well, thank you anyway,' I tell him.

But the next day it is the same. And the next. I am tired of starting my morning with a trip to the nearest public phone-box. I am tired of hearing the same tired engineer seem to commiserate. 'Has someone got it in for you?' he asks me. He makes it sound like a joke. I grow accustomed to the sight of the loose cable, dangling from the wall like a creeper.

But one morning there is no sign of any damage. The machine is unlit, the line is dead. But for once there is no visible vandalism. I go outside and follow the line of the cable all the way from its base to the point where it leaves the side of the building, just under the roof. There is no sign that anything has been tampered with. Oliver is at my elbow. 'Try the junction box,' he says.

'Have you got a screwdriver?'

'Here.'

I undo the screws one by one and prise the box open. Inside it the cable has been severed neatly, the two perfect ends barely a fraction of a centimetre apart.

Oliver whistles. 'Are you *sure* you haven't got any enemies?'

I try to think. Matthew? *Devlan?* Not after all this time, surely? But I shiver. I am still frightened of him. I touch Oliver on the shoulder. 'No good staying out here and getting cold,' I say. 'Let's go in. I suppose I'd better try to get hold of our trusty man again.'

The shirt has a hole in now. Still I take it to bed with me. Every night I pull it out from its place under my pillow and let it breathe.

Sometimes I even take it downstairs with me. It is there, a bundle of greying rag, on the coffee-table, on the draining-board, on the worktop, whenever I look round. The edges of the hole are fraying, with the collar. Sometimes there are stray white threads sticking to my clothing when I go out.

I try to draw their faces from memory – Devlan's, Simon's. But the results are laughable. And there are no photographs. Matthew's is the only one I have any success with, working from the snapshot I took on that first walk of ours, his red hair blazing against the autumn. Hunched over the kitchen table, I make sketch after sketch. Once I almost manage to capture the likeness and in my excitement I stand up suddenly, slopping my mug of coffee over the whole pile. The faces are spattered with brown stars. The table has a wet brown ring on it. Simon's old shirt is covered with little brown spots, like the trails of insects.

And now it is finally disintegrating. A few more months and it will be in pieces. Already there is a rent as big as my fist at the shoulder, where the stitching has snapped. Soon even the fabric itself will be worn to lace. Even now there are places where the threads are hardly stronger than cobwebs, held together only by some mysterious will to survive. The left elbow was rubbed thin even in Simon's time. Now if I put my hand down inside the sleeve I can see my own fingers.

And it is irreplaceable. I must try to patch it, before it gives out on me completely. I put a piece of paper over the worst hole and cut it to size. Then I find an old sheet and cut out a patch, as precise as I can make it. As I take out the pins I see that the piece of paper I have used is one of my own sketches. Matthew's imperfect features smile out at me, peppered with small holes. The skin at the outer corner of his right eye has been pierced twice by the same pin.

The phone would ring and I would rush to answer it, and then hang back, the receiver vibrating on its rest at my elbow. When I finally lifted it I wouldn't wait for Devlan to speak. I would drown out all his voices with a snatch of something musical of my own, before he could say he wasn't going to meet me. Or I would hold the phone at arm's length, waiting for him to call the tune.

The day he asked me to have lunch in his flat the city was grey with fog. He came in his car to collect us. As he drove through the suburbs the houses and gardens seemed to come at us out of nothing, meeting us for a moment and then receding. Further out, the animals had grazed knee-deep in grey fields. I turned round to look at Laura and Annie in the back of his car. Laura stared out at the mist. Annie had fallen asleep, her head on her chest, soft wisps of hair sticking to her cheek. On the other side of the glass the gardens were full of shadows. As we drove up to his entrance door, he looked at me sideways.

'Do you know,' he said, 'there's a tribe in Africa where they actually use gourds to stretch the women's vaginas? It's a kind of initiation-rite.'

'Yes?' I was laughing. 'There's always a tribe in Africa that

76

does everything you'd like to name. There's a tribe in Africa that . . .'

He interrupted me. 'We're here.'

We got out. He locked the car and unlocked the communal front door. We went up a wide concrete stairway to the first floor. A small typed card under glass next to one of the buttons said 'Devlan'. He fitted a second key in the lock and turned it.

The door swung open on a long, light room with big windows. A cardboard box of toys spilled its contents in the centre of the carpet. Annie staggered forward, waving her arms. 'Let me take your coats,' Devlan said. I let my anorak slip from my shoulders and handed it to him without touching his fingers.

'Where have the toys come from?'

'Oh . . .' He knelt on the floor to take the bald teddy Annie was holding out to him. 'They were Bethan's.'

'And you've kept them all?'

'Of course.' He looked surprised. 'It's her childhood. I wouldn't throw that away. Would you?'

I glanced down at Laura quiet and reserved beside me, her soft hair shining. She was still holding my hand. 'Perhaps not.'

'Sherry?'

'Yes. Thank you.'

He bent to get a bottle and two glasses out of a low cabinet to one side of the window. He frowned slightly as he filled the glasses almost to the rim. Then he straightened up. 'Cheers,' he said. 'There's squash, or orange juice. Would the kids like something? I'll just . . .'

There was a crash from the kitchen. Laura jumped violently. 'What's that?'

'Oh, don't worry,' Devlan said. 'It's nothing. Just the washing-machine. They're servicing it today.'

We ate our lunch to a background of bangs and crashes. Devlan found some leftover salad. I watched as he made sandwiches. He found some ice-cream in the back of the freezer for the girls. I remember how Annie ate it with the teddy-bear still clutched to her, half sliding from her lap. I stood up. From the kitchen the washing-machine still clicked and whirred. Testing. 'It must be just about time to go,' I said. 'I must just use your bathroom first.'

Devlan's bathroom was like any family bathroom, still slightly damp from the morning's showers, tooth-paste trailing across the wash-basin, cosmetics on shelves. I tried to guess which were Barbara's and which were his daughter's. When I unlocked the door he was standing with his back to me in another doorway. It was a room I hadn't seen. 'Come here.' He said it in a low voice, almost a whisper. He moved aside to let me come past him. We stood together in a small bedroom with one single bed. There was a black and white poster on the wall, a photograph of a very beautiful young man and a very beautiful young woman standing in a fountain. Her face was lifted to his. Her black hair was plastered to her skin. As their laughing mouths almost met the water ran off them both. Outside there was a view of other blocks of flats, and bare trees. The mist was clearing. 'This is Bethan's room,' he said. 'I shouldn't really be showing you.'

'Would she mind?'

'No. No . . . But . . .'

'Thank you for showing me,' I said. The mist shimmered like a flashback. 'What's the matter, darling?'

Annie was in the doorway, the teddy-bear's face pressed hard against the front of her pullover. Her cheeks had gone pink and blotchy.

'No, sweetheart,' I heard myself say to her. 'He has to stay here. He belongs to some other little girl. We can't take him away with us when we go.'

'We should go out for a meal,' I tell Matthew.

He is wary. 'Where would you like to go?'

'Oh, anywhere. Somewhere not too ... self-conscious. You choose.'

And he has chosen better than I could possibly have chosen for him. The café down by the bridge is crowded with teen-agers. The air is thick with gravy smells and smoke. The windows with their grimy collage of For Sale cards and bleached posters are opaque with steam.

He hands me the menu. It is coated in clear plastic, but even so the film of old grease is still visible. I can see my own fingerprints. 'Well, what shall we have?' He looks at me with a kind of malice.

I turn it over and read the back. Then I read it again. I hold it up in front of my face. 'I'll have sausage, egg and chips,' I say. 'With mushy peas.'

After a while an elderly man comes up and takes our order. He is Italian. At first we don't understand what he is asking of us. His whitish apron looks suspect. He is wiping his hands on a crumpled cloth.

He brings us our food and bangs it down on the table in front of us. 'Five pounds fifty.' He stands waiting as Matthew reaches into his pocket. But he hasn't any change.

'Here, let me. This is my treat,' I say. I wait for the old man to move away out of hearing. 'This reminds me of a bar I drank in once in Marseilles.'

'Yes?'

'Only that had sawn-off barrels, instead of proper chairs. And where the river is now there was the harbour. In fact ...' I am laughing. 'It wasn't much like this place at all.'

'When were you in Marseilles?'

'Oh, when I was quite young, hardly more than twenty. I spent a year there.'

'What were you doing?'

'Teaching. Illegally.'

'Illegally?'

'Well ... That makes it sound more glamorous than it was. I just didn't manage to get a work permit.'

79

'And didn't they turn you out? Didn't they see you were an undesirable alien?'

'I wasn't undesirable in those days.' I purse my mouth at him. Point scored. 'And they had more important things to think about.'

'Like?'

'Vice. And drugs. That night I was in the café someone got shot.'

'No kidding,' he says. The accent is ironic, as American as he can make it. 'And what part did you play in this *débâcle*?'

I have never seen him like this. 'I didn't play any part. We were all talking and drinking and then there were gun-shots and blood on the floor. Then, before we could even register what was happening, there were cops there with sub-machine-guns, ushering everyone out on to the street. And they had a couple of guys in hand-cuffs.'

Matthew looks at me suspiciously. 'You've never told me this before.'

'I've never remembered it before.' Suddenly I feel tired. 'Some affair of the heart.'

'Drugs, more likely. Anyway, they were two guys, you said.'

I open my mouth to say something and then think better of it. The mixture of grease and ketchup on my plate has cooled to a thin pinkish crust.

We finish our coffee and leave. Outside it is still raining. 'It's pissing down. Let me run you home,' I say, without conviction. He looks hunched and cold.

'No. Thanks. I'd rather walk.'

'Suit yourself.'

'Will I see you on Saturday as usual?'

'I don't think so. No.'

'Next week, then.'

'Probably not.'

'Right.' As I reverse almost towards him and brake suddenly to say goodbye it is not only his hair that is red but his whole body. In my mirror a red-eyed man stands on a red bridge and raises his red hand.

CHAPTER 5

WRESTLING FIGURES, UP to 2″ high, various ages and materials, up to £1 each.

SARAH, WHERE are you? Don't be afraid of Big Brother. Be brave and contact me.

KNIGHT, IMPRISONED in castle, 29, 5ft 10, slim, dark hair, seeks attractive damsel with talent for rescue.

WANTED, CIRCULAR SAW, hand or bench, price by agreement.

1949 MODEL, tax and MOT, good working order, average bodywork, wishes to meet female, gsoh. Please send photo.

TRANSCEIVER, VHF/UHF FM, ICOM IC3210 with hands-free mike and 12a PSU £245. Welz SP200 SWR/PWR Meter £25. Pair 14′ ELE 2M Yagis with power splitter, co-ax, ally pole and wall brackets £40. VHF and UHF Co-Linears, Co-Ax and Welz changeover switch £30, or altogether £320.

SPIRAL STAIRCASE, WOODEN treads on steel frame, excellent condition, £295.

After a gap of years I met Devlan for lunch at the Gate Wine Bar. It was just before Christmas. As I took my scarf and beret off I caught sight of myself in a mirror. My cheeks were pink with the cold, my eyes shining. He turned from the bar and saw me. 'Oh, hello . . .' he said. Then, 'You look really . . .'

'Thank you.'

'Can I get you something to drink?'

'A dry white wine, please.'

We sat down. He leaned back, smiling with his eyes. 'It's good to see you.'

'And you,' I said. 'How's the linear development going?'

We talked. For once, we talked. About his life. About mine. Then he said, 'I saw this play on television the other night. It reminded me of you.'

There was a silence. I twisted the stem of the wineglass between my fingers. 'What was it about?'

'Oh . . . About this couple, who were having a sort of long-term affair. They only saw each other once every few years.'

'Mmm.'

'They just carried this thing on slowly between them for half their lives with one meeting about every five years.'

'Like a kind of distance learning?' I suggested. 'Did they write, at least?'

He shook his head. He seemed quite serious. 'They never wrote anything. They hardly even said anything. That was half the secret.'

'What do you mean?'

'That was how they could carry on for so long, caring about each other.'

'What was the other half?' In spite of myself I had begun to smile.

He raised his glass then, and looked at me. 'To the next five years,' he said.

We talked so often about Bethan. Perhaps she was the only thing we *could* talk about. 'How's Bethan?' I would ask him, and he would start to tell me.

'You love her more than anyone, don't you?' I said once. 'She's the only one you've ever really cared for.'

He didn't deny it. He was impassive, staring out at the slow ribbon of the by-pass as it uncoiled between waterlogged fields. His hands tightened slightly on the steering-wheel as he went to overtake. We drew abreast with the flapping tarpaulin sides of the lorry and for a long time we stayed there, as the wind cracked and worried at the ropes. At last he pulled back into the slow lane. Then he said, 'I often wish I'd had more children.'

'You still could,' I said.

He didn't say anything. Barbara was the same age as he was.

'You still could,' I said again.

There was a long silence. Then he said, 'I hear what you're saying.'

'I always wanted . . .' I said. 'What I always . . .'

He took his eyes from the road for a moment to glance at me. 'What?' he said. 'What did you want?'

I took a deep breath, but my voice still wouldn't stay quite level. 'I don't know. When I was expecting Annie, I thought . . .' I tried again. 'Men say that pregnant women look stupid and ugly, like cows or buses. But I didn't *feel* ugly. I felt beautiful and erotic in a way I'd never even thought of. And I began to see the other women differently too. And I thought, what a waste, for men not to know, not to realise . . . And I was always looking for someone who could share that. But Simon . . .'

My voice shook. 'But Simon?' he prompted me.

The fields on either side of the road had gone silver with

86

the light from the sky. I blinked hard to stop the tears from running down my face. I could taste salt. I laughed. 'I haven't yet found anyone who can understand that,' I said.

'Well, you haven't found one here either,' Devlan said. He laughed with me. 'I'm afraid I find a pregnant woman as grotesque as the next man.'

Once we talked about age. Devlan's hand was across the top of my dining-table. 'Of course, it's a bit different when you haven't lived through the war,' he said. 'You haven't got the same perspective.'

'I'm not sure I want that particular perspective,' I said.

'There were whole years when we didn't have any formal education at all. I expect you find that hard to imagine.'

'It must have been tough.'

'We had to learn what we could from what we saw going on around us.'

'Like what?' I said.

'Oh . . .' He shrugged. 'Kids running wild, fathers not ever there, or not coming back, whole streets disappearing overnight.'

'Weren't you frightened to be alive?'

He shook his head. 'It was a great time, actually. We could get away with anything. We were natural entrepreneurs. We found ways of getting whatever we wanted.'

'You must miss that,' I said.

He didn't seem to hear me. He sighed. 'But you end up feeling you're weighed down with almost too much experience. You can see through everything. You understand it all too well.'

'Tough,' I said again.

He looked at his hand, turning it over and bending and flexing the fingers. 'As a woman, you must be acutely aware of the pressures of ageing,' he said.

I raised my head and stared at him. 'No. I don't think I am.'

'Women usually get pretty up-tight about the prospect of losing their looks.'

I blink. I hear myself say, 'I suppose it depends what they look like to start with.'

'Of course,' he says easily. 'With your physical type and bone-structure . . . I can imagine you looking almost the same at seventy as you do now.'

Once we were saying goodbye. 'Next week, then,' Devlan was saying. 'Though I've got a lot on at the moment. I'm not absolutely sure I'll be able to make it. I probably will. I will if I can. And I'll phone you if I can't.'

Was that it? I hardly heard what he was saying. I followed him to my front door.

'So I'll ring you,' he said again. We were standing in the hall. 'I'll let you know, one way or the other.'

I couldn't speak. There was a white thread dangling from his elbow.

'What is it? What's the matter?' He reached out and ruffled my hair. I took a step backwards. His other hand was on the doorknob.

The thread hung there, clearly visible. I couldn't say anything. I couldn't reach out and touch even his jacket.

He opened the door and took a step backwards. He stood there on the top step for a moment, silhouetted against the wall of the house opposite. Then he half turned and began to go down.

From the doorway I called out after him, 'You've got a piece of white cotton stuck to your left sleeve.'

'What? Oh . . .' He turned his arm over, searching. 'Oh, yes.' He flicked it away into the well of our steep front garden. 'Thanks.' He looked back at me then and laughed.

'I'm setting up a reading at the shop next month,' I tell Matthew. 'Will you come?'

'What kind of reading? Poetry? You know I'm not very interested in all that.'

'Not poetry. Something a bit more immediate and universal. It's the first time I've done anything like this, and I wanted to get someone who would bring in a proper audience.'

'Like who? Marinda Darouche?'

' "She wrapped her cloak round her more tightly as he lifted her in his arms and placed her gently on the saddle. She clung to him as the shouts grew nearer. The distant hills shimmered already in the light of first dawn"? There are a lot of lonely old ladies who swear by her. It might be worth a try. But actually, I was thinking of a travel writer. Something to shake them up a bit.'

'From Juneau to Maui by exercise bike?'

'Something like that.'

'Will he be funny?'

'Who said anything about a "he"?'

It takes me several weeks to set it up – the writer and the publicity. Oliver helps me tape up posters in the shop window. Copies of the writer's latest book are tastefully arranged in front of them. We even manage to get hold of a photograph from somewhere: Helen Quinnell welcomes potential customers from the doorway of a straw hut, her walking shorts crumpled and dirty, her sunglasses slightly askew. She is smiling. I ring up the man at the *Messenger* and beg him to put in a short paragraph. I send out invitations. I go to Oddbins and choose bottles of wine.

'Have you decided yet whether or not you intend to come?' I ask Matthew.

'I might.' He says it grudgingly.

'I'm taking her for a meal afterwards, before I drive her to the station. She's bringing a friend. And I've asked Oliver to join us. You could come too, if you wanted.'

'I'm not sure. I'll see how I feel.'

We are in the shop. A small sheaf of biographical leaflets lies beside me on a low table. 'Helen Quinnell has been involved in exploration and travel of one form or another since her early teens . . .' I brush against them and they slide to the floor, spreading themselves in a fan over the carpet. I kneel to pick them up. Matthew is down on the floor beside me. He grins at me from between table-legs. He is holding one of the leaflets. 'Can't say I like the sound of her much.'

'Well, you just tip me the wink,' I say, 'when you're sure you've decided.'

There was the night Devlan drove back by a circuitous route. It was a part of the city I didn't recognise. The buildings seemed taller, drabber, more functional. Litter drifted across the pavements, flapped on the road in front of us, got caught under the wheels. These streets we drove through were streets I had never seen. The shop-fronts were badly lit, a jumble of price-tags and ethnic menus and shrivelled cheese-plants. People with turned-up collars were hurrying home. In the end-of-evening traffic our car hardly moved.

'Do you see that building just ahead of us?' We were stopped at a light. I could see a tall shabby structure with rows of uniform rectangular windows. Every floor was lit up.

'Yes,' I said to him.

'It's a hospital. It's where my father died. Do you see that window up there? Second row down, third from the end?'

'Yes,' I said. Through the glass of the car window the pedestrians were still coming and going in the half-dark, their mouths opening and closing like the mouths of fish. 'Was it . . . Was he . . . Did he have a long illness?'

'Not all that long. A few weeks.'

'And how did you . . .?'

Devlan grunted. It was a kind of laugh. 'It's all right. It's over three years ago now. You know . . .' He hesitated. 'Though it still feels odd sometimes to think he's not alive any more. He had a kind of authority. We always thought of him as indestructible.'

I reached across the gear-stick to where his left hand rested on his thigh. 'But it comes to us all,' he said. He turned to look at me, the whites of his eyes slightly pink in the glow from the light. I watched his features flick from red through flame and amber. When they turned green I let go of his hand.

I showed him a story I wrote once. A woman in labour was hallucinating about the trench fighting of the First World War. It made him angry.

'You can't do this!' He picked up the sheaf of paper from the dashboard and shook it in my face. 'You don't have the faintest understanding . . . Young men losing their lives, that's not something you can talk about in the same breath as some woman wittering on over a belly the size of a cement-mixer.'

I kept my voice steady. 'Why not?' I asked him.

'Because . . .' He enumerated the reasons. Then he seemed to calm down. He shrugged.

'So can I have my story back?'

He gave it to me. It was dog-eared, the print blurred grey with the pressure of his thumb. 'It's good therapy, though.' He was smiling now. 'You must make sure you keep up this writing. Anything that makes you feel better, that helps you to manage . . .'

'I'm not interested in managing anyone,' I said.

'The trouble with you,' Devlan said, 'is that you're unable to feel guilty.'

'Should I feel guilty?'

He pushed back hard against the seat, his head pressing on the head-rest. The muscles of his neck strained and then relaxed. 'Everyone lives either on the guilt axis or on the shame axis. It's impossible to live on both.'

I tried to copy his voice, the tone, the intonation, even the shape of the vowels. 'And what about you? Which do you live by?' I asked him. I turned my head to look out of the window. We were nearly at the end of the journey. On their bare hill, the pines were already coming into view.

We were talking about fathers. He said something under his breath. I couldn't ask him to repeat it. There was a big stripe of shadow across the centre of his face, cast by a telegraph-pole, or a branch. 'None of us ever really knew,' he said.

'What? That he was going to die?' I could hear his breathing, heavy and deliberate, like someone on the telephone. I rephrased it. 'How long he was going to go on living?'

He turned to face me. The whites of his eyes were pink in the pink haze from the town. 'And what about your father?' he said. His voice was so low I had to imagine the words.

'My father? What about him?'

'Is he still alive?'

'Yes. Of course he is.' I say it again, as if to convince myself. 'Of course he is.'

'And you're very fond of him.'

'Ha!' The tone of my voice surprised me. I stared out of the car window, at the high blank eyes of a hospital, the yellow gleam from the wards spilling out into the street. Everything the light touched looked tarnished. 'No, I'm not fond of him. Not now. I hate him, as a matter of fact.'

Devlan glanced across at me mildly, half smiling. 'That's a great pity,' he said.

One night I asked Devlan to drive to a place I knew. He didn't ask any questions. 'Just over there,' I said. 'On the other side of the green, in front of the church. There, under those trees.'

He drove the car slowly to where I pointed, and parked. He turned off the engine. The metal parts ticked as they cooled. It was quite dark. There was only the moon to outline the tops of the trees in silver, to pick out the posts of the chain-link fence that circled the cricket green on this side. His face was invisible. 'Well?' he said.

'I want to take a photograph.'

I can't remember what he said. 'There isn't any light'? 'You haven't got a camera'?

'Give me your hand.'

He didn't protest.

And for a long time we sat there. I felt his hand, the dry warm flesh of his wrist. I ran my fingers over his skin until I was sure I could never forget. I told myself this was what it felt like to be old – what my own skin would feel like to someone else when I was old.

'You lead such a *safe* life,' Devlan said to me once.

'Do I?'

'House, husband, children – what could be safer than that?'

'You've got a wife and child. And a flat.'

'That's not the same thing.'

'*Ah* . . .' I thought of my life, the line that went nowhere. 'It might be possible to take risks by telling people about it,' I said.

'Telling people? Writing about it, you mean? Where's the danger in that? That isn't where the real risk is.'

'Where is the real risk?'

He raised an eyebrow. 'The real risk is when men get together and hundreds of thousands of pounds change hands.'

I looked at him. 'I haven't got hundreds of thousands of pounds. I haven't even got hundreds. I've only got a husband, and children, and half a house.'

I step outside the back door of the shop and look up at the sky. It is going to be a fine evening. Already the temperature has dropped several degrees since lunchtime. It smells like frost. The sky is clear and cloudless, lit near the horizon with a pinkish glow from the lights of the town, too full of light for me to see stars. I take a deep breath of cold air. My face is stinging. When I move to go back in my skirt is cold against my legs.

Inside, Oliver is talking to someone. She has arrived already.

93

Helen Quinnell bends to pick up one of the leaflets. I watch as her eyes dart over it. She folds it in half and puts it in the slim leather bag she is wearing slung over one shoulder. Then she looks up at me and smiles.

'You must be Jan Hickman?'

I hold out my hand. 'Helen Quinnell, I presume?'

She laughs at the old joke. I like her. 'Do you know it was harder to get here than to fly to Delhi last September?'

'I can imagine.'

'The train itself was quite an experience. Then there was a bus between Wetheringden and Hatchworth. And the man in the seat next to me kept clearing his throat and gobbing on the floor.'

'I'm sorry. I did hear about the bus, but I'd forgotten. There was a landslip there a couple of weeks ago. We've had so much rain. But it seems to have decided to clear up at last.'

'Except for the phlegm,' she says. She makes a face.

'I didn't think you travel writers were allowed to be squeamish.'

'No. We're not. It's all thoroughly macho.' She laughs again. 'Which is why I make a point of it. Fashion has it that to be effective we've got to be desensitised. But it's nonsense. You might as well let yourself be rolled down river inside a barrel. You may get there. But if you don't let yourself suffer, you don't really find out much.'

'Yes?' It's then that I look past her and see a woman standing just behind her, almost at her elbow. I look at Helen enquiringly.

Her eyes are very blue in her brown face. She brushes a wisp of dry fair hair out of them. 'Oh . . . Let me introduce you to . . . This is Cath. She always comes with me to readings. Not on my travels. But to the rough stuff.' She laughs again.

Cath smiles. 'I only come because you want me to.' She is round and dumpy, perhaps older. I look at Helen again, at the small lines round her eyes. Perhaps not. Cath puts an arm round her shoulders. 'Sometimes I bring my knitting.'

'Does it make you nervous?'

'Incredibly nervous. Isn't it stupid? It's her life, after all. And she can handle it, anyone can see that.'

I try to gauge the tone, but something is escaping me, something I have no access to. 'Let me get you both a glass of wine,' I say. Oliver is somewhere behind me, in the kitchen. 'Oliver?'

He comes through the doorway behind me, holding a cork-screw. 'Would you like to open one of these bottles?'

'Sure.' He looks at Cath, then at Helen. He addresses Helen. 'White, or red?'

'Red will be fine.'

He sinks the screw into the cork until the two arms raise themselves into the air. The metal spike has entered at a slight angle, splintering the cork at the point of exit. 'Sorry about that.' He shrugs. Then he grips the bottle between his knees and presses down slowly.

The shop fills up gradually. It is quite a good turn-out. There must be thirty or forty people. I glance at Helen next to me. Under the unseasonable tan she has gone pale. 'Is it time, do you think?' She nods. I walk out to the front and turn to address them.

The shop is packed. From the back I hadn't realised just how full it was. The folding seats we've borrowed from the library are all taken. People are standing at the back, leaning against the shelves, blocking the doorway. I scan the faces. Most of them are familiar. But not all of them. Where have these people come from? Many of them seem to be young, younger than almost all our regular customers. A cluster of sharp jeaned knees sticks up from one corner. Books are being passed from hand to hand.

I don't see Matthew anywhere. Perhaps after all he has decided not to come. 'I can honestly say that it's a great personal pleasure to me to be able to introduce . . .' I begin.

*

She reads well. Without a trace of self-importance. But slowly, with obvious quiet enjoyment, tasting the words. And the atmosphere is suddenly oddly intimate. It isn't like a poet reading, or a journalist. It is like a woman reading her own diary, writing her own diary aloud. And yet we are not embarrassed. The strangeness and danger of what she does are never explicit. We are never asked to empathise. And yet the empathy is there, tangible, in the spaces she has left between the words. I stand at the back, sipping the wine in my glass slowly, forgetting who I am, forgetting that I am responsible for all this. I hear her soft voice describing a mountain landscape, joking with the indigenous guides, tangling with taboos, and surviving. And I am elsewhere, in a small room in the darkness more than ten years ago, my back against the wall.

'Now . . .' Helen puts her book down on the table at her elbow and picks up her glass of wine. She takes a mouthful, looking over the rim at the waiting faces. 'I'm so grateful to you for coming and listening to me with such attention. You really are extraordinary.'

The audience laughs.

'I know. I'm not supposed to say that. I'll shut up. It's your turn. Would anyone like to ask me any questions?'

For an awkward moment there is silence. I prepare myself to rush in. My mouth has gone suddenly dry. Then a child in the second row puts up her hand.

'Yes?'

'Do you have any pets?'

Helen understands at once what she is asking. 'No, I don't. Though I do love animals. But you see I couldn't take them with me. And I don't like the thought of off-loading my responsibilities on to someone else. So I have to be content to make friends with the animals I meet along the way.' She smiles. 'A marmot actually came up and sniffed inside the entrance of my tent once. And there are donkeys, of course. But you can't make friends with donkeys. It's up to *them* to decide whether or not they're prepared to put up with *you!*' The child sits back in her seat, obviously happy, squirming slightly.

Cath raises her hand.

'Yes?'

'Do you ever get lonely?'

Helen laughs. She seems to be always laughing. She has heard that one before. 'Of course I do. Next?'

Before I am properly aware of what I am doing I have raised my hand. A few other hands have gone up as well, now. The audience is beginning to relax again. One or two people are half rising from their seats with impatience. But I am the one Helen points to. 'Jan?'

'This is going to sound really frivolous . . .'

'Don't be defensive. No question can be frivolous. And no one at one of my readings is allowed to apologise. Right?'

'Right.' But I feel myself going red. The heat rises from my neck to my cheeks and into the roots of my hair. 'I just wondered . . .' I am stammering. 'I wondered about the men.'

'What men?'

'The men. All the men. The men you travel with, the men you set things up with, the men who guide you through the passes. All of them.'

She says patiently, 'What about them? I'm not sure I . . .'

'Isn't it impossible to communicate with them?' I have said it now. 'And aren't you frightened?'

'Impossible, no, not completely. Though . . .' her eyes meet Cath's, 'I've had to learn a number of quite difficult languages. But frightened, yes. I'm always frightened. And with good reason.'

'What kind of reason?'

It is a male voice, from somewhere near the door. People in the audience are turning round in their seats to see who it is. I look across them and see Matthew's hair gleaming in a crowd of heads. No one says anything. The silence drags on. Thirty seconds. A minute. The people who are sitting down

97

begin to fidget in their seats. Helen Quinnell stands looking at the carpet as if she has forgotten where she is. Then she looks up, searching in the sea of faces. 'I can't see you,' she says. 'Can you come forward? Can I see who I'm talking to, before I try to answer that?'

But Matthew has gone. I feel a sudden draught of cold from the door. More people are turning their heads, rustling their belongings. Then gradually the room settles back into silence. Helen sits down and smooths her skirt. 'Shall I just tell you a bit about the new journey I'm planning to do this coming spring?' she says.

By now the people are dispersing, clutching their signed books under their arms, clicking their tongues in admiration. In the back kitchen Oliver is rinsing out glasses. 'Thank you so much for that marvellous reading,' I am saying. 'And I must say I thought it was so good the way you fielded . . .'

'It's all right. It happens.' She reaches for my hand and squeezes it. It feels impulsive. Then I look up and see Matthew.

He is standing a few feet away from us, outside her range of vision. He pulls a face. I am trying hard not to laugh. 'I hope you'll let us treat you both to supper,' I say.

'Oh. Yes, of course. That would be lovely.' Again she glances at Cath for corroboration. Cath nods.

'And let me introduce you to a friend of mine. Matthew Donaldson.'

'Hello. Nice to meet you. Are you coming with us?'

'Yes. He is,' I say quickly. 'Matthew was at the reading. He's quite an admirer of yours.'

'Really?' She looks amused. She doesn't believe me. 'Admirers are so hard to come by these days, especially male ones. Do tell me your name again.'

'Matthew,' he says.

They look at each other for what seems a long moment. Then she says, 'Ah.'

*

As we leave the shop I catch sight of myself in the glass. A tune is going through my head, one of the tracks we relax to at the end of the aerobics class.

> *The art of melancholy,*
> *I've really got it down,*
> *The art of melancholy*
> *Sealed with a frown.*

I straighten my back. My image straightens its back with me. *Shoulders down, knees slightly bent. DON'T LET THAT RIGHT KNEE ROLL IN. AND recover. HOLD THE ANKLE, NOT THE TOE. LOOK AT SOMETHING STRAIGHT AHEAD OF YOU.* I look at something straight ahead of me. It is myself.

'Perhaps you should . . .' he said in the dark car once.

'What?'

'Cut through it all somehow. Take me by surprise. *Make* me . . .'

'You mean you want me to *seduce* you?'

He stumbled slightly over the words, as if they were foreign, or painful. 'I mean, cut through . . . all this bullshit. I don't know . . . When I think of all the people I carry round with me . . .'

'Am I one of the people you carry round with you?'

His voice was several tones lower than usual. 'Yes.'

There was a long silence. I couldn't look at him. The shadow of the steering-wheel was across his hand.

'You don't want me,' I said.

'I suppose I don't want . . . the package.'

'You don't love me.' I heard my own voice saying the absurd sentence. It was like talking in my sleep. It had a kind of necessity.

'I do love you.' His was hardly recognisable. I wondered if he was going to cry. 'In a way.'

I didn't laugh. 'What, then?'

'I'm frightened.'

'Yes,' I said. My teeth had started to chatter. I released the seat-belt and opened the car door.

Inside, the house was quite silent. The hall light had been left on, but the upstairs rooms were in darkness. I could almost hear them breathing – Laura, Annie, Simon. I stepped through the open door into the sitting-room and stood looking through the gap in the curtains at a strip of wet street, gleaming in the glow from the streetlamp just outside. I heard Devlan start his engine and drive away. Then I let myself slide to the floor.

I sat with my back against the dividing wall. Through the wool of my sweater I could feel the faint give of the cork tiles. Between the half-open curtains a turning white beam picked out the pattern of the paper on the other wall, just over my left shoulder. Gradually my eyes got used to the blackness, until I could make out every detail of the small room, the puckered cloth of the couch, the screws in the bookcase. A child's book left open on the floor, its spine cracking with the strain. An old pullover of Simon's sprawled over the back of a chair. The ribbing of my own socks. For half an hour I sat in the dark without moving, as the wrinkled wool at my ankles came and went in the orange light, in and out of focus. Where was she now, the one who did it with her socks on? Were the pills still lined up beside her bed in a neat pattern? And had her toes curled in that same old reflex, the night she had wanted to die?

We were driving home. Devlan was talking about his years in the army, just after the war. There was nostalgia in his voice. 'Of course, you're too young to remember all that,' he said.

My father had been in the army, at Monte Cassino. 'Yes,' I said. 'By the time I grew up they weren't doing military service any more.'

'Pity.'

'Not that it would have affected me much. At that age I was still into writing my diary and climbing trees.'

'And I was into Bobby Mackinley,' he said.

The name meant nothing to me. Was it a singer? A football player? Someone he had grown up with? His eyes were on the road, the ribbon of darkness uncurling ahead of us, pierced in places by pairs of moving lights. 'Trees and diaries have their uses,' I said.

> La, la, la, je ne l'ose, je ne l'ose dire,
> La, la, la, je le vous diray.
> Il est ung homme en no ville
> Qui de sa femme est jaloux.
> Il n'est pas jaloux sans cause
> Mais il est cocu du tout.
> La, la, la, je ne l'ose, je ne l'ose dire,
> La, la, la, je le vous diray.

'I hope you'll like this place.' I reach for my napkin and unfold it. I spread it on my lap. 'Anyway, it's about the best a town like this can do.'

'But I love Italian food!' Helen picks up the menu and turns the pages. 'And stop being defensive. I've already had to take you to task once about that. And I love everything. Well, almost . . . I'm terribly accommodating.' She is speaking to me. But over the top of the mock-leather folder she is looking hard at Matthew.

'Even the men?' he says. Behind the frame of his glasses his raised eyebrow has made itself invisible.

I kick him under the table and the crockery shudders. No one seems to notice. 'I think I'll have a pint of lager, while we're waiting,' Cath says.

'And me.' Oliver lays his menu on the table and leans back in his chair, looking at the ceiling. 'Jan, tell me what to have.'

'Don't be silly.'

'Then I'll have the steak and chips. I warn you.'

'You can have steak and chips if you like.'

'Do I like?'

I pretend to hit him across the face with the menu. 'What's the matter, Oliver, for heaven's sake? You can't be as tired as all that! Just shut up and choose something. Otherwise you'll get the crappo ai quattro formaggi. And lump it.'

It is Helen's turn to look uncomfortable. 'Listen, you guys. Could we cool it just a tad?' Then the voice changes. 'Or they'll be calling out the local constabulary.'

Matthew's voice cuts through. 'And this whole place will be swarming with men.'

'With whom at times it is almost impossible to communicate.' Helen narrows her eyes at him and raises her glass.

There is a silence. The waiter has come to take our orders. When he is out of earshot, Matthew looks across at Helen and says, 'Tell us more about what you do.'

'The writing, or the travelling?'

'The travelling.'

'Well . . .' She is playing with her napkin on the table, rolling and unrolling one corner between her thumb and middle finger. 'That's quite a large question. What do you want to know?'

'What first made you do it?'

'Go off on my own, you mean?'

'Yes. It always seems such an enormous step to take, to leave . . .'

'Well, actually, I didn't have all that much to leave. I was working free-lance. In a sense I was taking my work with me. And I wasn't in a serious relationship, there wasn't anyone I was leaving behind.'

'Were there times when you were in real danger?'

'Oh . . . I've often wondered. None of it seemed dangerous at the time. But afterwards, when I got to think about it all, yes. There was a horse that bolted on a mountain path, between walls of rock, and I lost both my stirrups. There was the time I was walking on my own in the mountains in Corsica and I heard someone whistle. And the whistle was answered by someone on the other side of the valley. And before I knew it the whole place was full of whistles, echoing all round me, and I was at the centre of the whistling. That was pretty hairy. And there was the time in Petra when one of the young guys was blocking my way out and all I could see was the shape of his body against the light, and I knew what he was doing.'

'That must have been unnerving,' I say.

'Well, only afterwards, when I had the leisure to think about it. At the time I just did whatever you do do – hung on, told myself not to panic, put my head down and kept on walking. You're not immune, you know, just because you decide to think of yourself as a certain kind of person, the kind who does things. Deciding almost makes it worse.'

The waiter comes back and puts our food in front of us. 'I think I must need this,' I say. I'm shivering. I turn to Matthew. 'What did you choose?'

As we eat the conversation fragments. Oliver is talking to Cath, with obvious interest. Matthew and I still quiz Helen. She is looking tired now, the flush of the wine making her traveller's skin look almost yellow.

Matthew brings his knife and fork together on his plate and leans back. Then he says, 'You still haven't really told us.'

'Told you what?' Helen almost barks it at him. Cath shifts in her chair.

'What it was.'

'What what was?'

'What they did to you. What we did to you. What have we ever done?'

I put my hand on his arm. 'Matthew, I don't . . .'

'It wasn't just the man in the ruins. There was something else, wasn't there, something that wasn't so easy to forget? What was it? Did a bandit come out of the *maquis* and threaten you at knife-point? Did one of those Tibetan guides rape you, or something, between checkpoints?'

But she looks at him coolly. 'What makes you think there was anything?'

'A woman like you . . . There must have been. All that ice, and the wind whistling under the brailing. Hats off to him, whatever he did, that's what I say!'

'Matthew . . .' I reach up to stroke his hair.

But he ducks and shakes me off. He has had enough. He feels in his pocket and brings out a handful of notes and loose change. He counts out enough to pay for what he ordered and piles it in the centre of the table. His coat is hanging from the back of his chair. He pulls it off roughly and slings it over his shoulder, his finger curled through the loop at the neck. 'Well, I'll see you. And thanks.' He turns to take a last look at Helen. 'Enjoy.' It is the same accent she used. Then the door-handle crashes back against the wall and he is gone.

One night we went for a walk on the common. What did Devlan say to me? I can't remember. What did I say to him? We sat on a bench in the darkness between high trees. He bent to look into my face. 'I thought you were tougher than this,' I think he said.

'What do you mean, tougher?'

'I thought you could take this kind of thing and shrug it off.'

'I'm not tough,' I said. 'Resilient. But not tough.'

'Perhaps that's what I mean.'

We stood up. For a long time we stayed there on the path with our arms round each other, not speaking. I could make out the branches over his shoulder, the paler face of the sky. I breathed in the smell of his jacket in the dark. Then he tightened his arms round me and lifted me from the ground, until my eyes were just level with his.

When I get back to the cottage it is quite dark. There is only the moonlight, sliding across the backs of the furniture and dripping on to the floor in white pools. I curl up on the sofa and close my eyes, but they come open again. Something wet oozes out from between my eyelashes. I sit staring out at the dark trees on the other side of the window, and hear the wind in the wires. Beside me, something white. Simon's shirt. I pick it up and wrap it tightly round my hand until I can't feel my fingers.

Somewhere I hear an owl. Or a cat. Or a child crying. But there are no children. Then the flat thud of the post dropping on the mat. Sun streams in across the carpet, across my legs, still covered by yesterday's creased skirt. Around me on the floor, on the arms of the sofa, trailing from the cushions to the rug, white ribbons. They are everywhere. Festoons of them hang from the coffee table, cling to my clothes. There is even one drooping from the lampshade, slightly singed at one end. When I stretch and stand up to go into the kitchen and fill the kettle, white threads stick to me all over like so many blades of grass.

CHAPTER 6

TO ALL females, 25–45, I call myself a sensitive, caring male who is loyal, honest and looking for a permanent relationship. Not much tooffer, only myself.

GOOD QUALITY FOAM padded gun bags, two (room for scope) £30 the pair, or split, £17 each.

WINE BOTTLE HOLDER, wrought iron, reminiscent large birdcage, 4ft 6in tall, distinctive feature, £300.

STUFFED BARN OWLS, pair, no question of splitting, immaculate, offers in region of £600.

ZEBEDEE'S SPRING sprung, roundabout lost it's magic. Dougal in search of pastures new. Florence, are you out there?

CRASH HELMET, RED, good make, visor, boxed, unwanted gift, £15.

I step outside the door of my cottage and breathe in the pure cold. The superimposed layers of bare vegetation fall away steeply, each fold outlined in frost. Down there is the river. I can't see it, but even at this temperature I can smell its presence. And on the other side the land rises again steeply towards the Scotch pines. There is a moon now, just above them, white and huge, blotting out a possibility of stars. The whole surface of the path in front of me is picked out in silver. A couple of inches from my foot a white pebble gleams like a gobbet of phlegm.

This week the aerobics class is harder. The sweat is running off me. I can't keep going. I leave my place and go to the water fountain for a drink. I stay there as long as I decently can, bent over the jet of cold water, my heart pounding. Then I straighten up and wipe my mouth on my arm. *Half-stars. Four on the right. Four on the left.* They have started on the cool-down. I thread my way back through them and take up my old position. The tall thin woman in front of me has a new outfit, a bold Y of red over a brief grey top and grey cycling shorts. Between them her skin flexes and crinkles symmetrically like gold wings.

Much later Devlan told me, 'There was one who lay on the floor and kicked and screamed.'

'Why did she do that?'

'How should I know? She was crazy. She wanted me to do something, and I didn't do it. She was out of her mind. She must have been, to lie on the floor and scream.'

'What did she want you to do?' I asked him.

We are lying on the floor, side on to the glass, our teacher walking carefully between us. She corrects an elbow here, the angle of an ankle there, puts her hand on muscle to illustrate some imperfection. In the mirror she is walking in my direction. She bends down to me and tugs at my arm. 'Can you lift your head up a bit more? Like this?' She gets down on the floor to show me.

I try it. 'No. I'm afraid I can't.'

'Are you sure?'

'I'm not that flexible. I think I'm too old.'

'Oh, well. Never mind. Just do what you feel comfortable with.'

I carry on, raising my leg steadily, forcing my mind blank, overriding the growing ache in my thigh. And then the class is almost over. We are on our backs, one knee clutched to our chests. *AND expand that leg-muscle. If it starts shaking ease off slightly. As soon as it relaxes, see if you can take it a bit further.* She is looking in my direction again. *IF IT STARTS SHAKING . . .*

We lie back on our mats, looking at the ceiling.

> *The art of melancholy,*
> *I've really got it down.*

The sweat trickles down my face, round the edges of my eye-sockets and into my hair.

I think about the woman who lay on the floor and screamed. Why did she scream? Could I have screamed with her? How would we have sounded, with our duet of screaming, the whole building vibrating as we pounded the floorboards with our feet? How much noise could the two of us have made?

There was one who gave as good as she got. 'She told me to stop bullshitting her, to stop off-loading all my . . .'

'Really?'

He chuckled. 'I only rang to ask her a small favour and she . . .' He was smiling.

'What?'

'Told me where I could put it. And when I pointed out that she was behaving quite irrationally, she told me to fuck off.'

'Just fuck off, like that?'

'Who did I think I was kidding? And that I was the one who was screwed up.'

I frowned. 'Has it ever occurred to you that perhaps you are?'

'Rubbish. How could I be?' He was laughing again, using the boyish voice. 'She's the one. She actually told me to fuck off! I heard her.'

'How did she say it, exactly?' I asked him.

'At least they're all different.'

'What do you mean?'

The tip of Deborah's red pen hovers over one advertisement, makes an inscrutable symbol in the margin, and moves on. 'Well, not absolutely identical. You know. You'd think they'd all be worded exactly the same. But each one somehow finds a way to express her need in a slightly original way.'

'*Her* need?'

'Or his need.'

I grunt. 'I'd rather they were identical,' I tell her. 'It would be more honest.'

'Like a chorus line. Just waiting for some gorgeous hunk to pick you out.' She makes the fingers of her left hand into a doll shape and skips them across the table-top towards me. The little legs kick up. Then the hand collapses. She rests her chin on those same fingers. 'Or majorettes,' she says.

'I hate majorettes.'

'You don't? How can you? All those tossing fringes and glistening silver – '

'Oh, shut up!'

She bites her lip and goes back to the reading. Then I see the red pen swoop down again. 'Hey, listen to this one! "Advanced baton-twirler with perfect timing wltm . . ." '

Before I know what I am doing I have reached out my foot to kick her hard under the table. 'Shut up, Debbie!' I say again.

She stands up and puts her arm round me. 'Hey!' she says. 'I didn't . . .' Her two hands on my shoulders shake me, very gently. 'Hey!' she says again. 'Hey!'

It has snowed. It does snow early sometimes, even in this part of the world, even before Christmas. But when I draw up at Deborah's front door she runs out to meet me in her slippers. 'Hey!' she says. 'Guess what?'

'What?'

'I've met a new man!'

'A New Man? What, one of the ones who do the washing-up?'

She laughs. 'That would be too much. But he is a man. And he is new – to me, at least.'

'Good,' I say. 'Great. Perhaps he *will* do the washing-up, once you've got him in shape. You can try, anyway. What's his name?'

'Sean.'

'That's unobjectionable. What's he like?'

'Oh . . .' Deborah shifts from foot to foot. The snow is melting and seeping through to her socks. 'He's lovely. You'll see. I've invited him over on New Year's Eve. You'll come, won't you, with Matthew? Then you'll see what he's like. He's very new. Quite unlike anyone I've ever met. And almost unbelievably manly.'

'How did you meet him?'

'You're not going to believe this.'

'Through one of those ads, don't tell me.'

'Yes. I called the number. And I liked the voice. He had a nice voice.'

I hesitate. 'Not Spring is Sprung? Not Zebedee from the Roundabout?'

'The one without much tooffer,' she says. But she is laughing.

'How old is he?'

'Oh, I don't know. It's hard to tell exactly. Forty? Fifty?'

'Married?'

'Probably.'

'Be careful,' I say to her as I hand over the package of books she ordered. 'You don't have to tell me about those.'

I drive back along the lanes. Already the snow is melting, sliding from branches and landing in front of the car with a soft thud. The bonnet of the Mini is spattered with snow. The sweep of the wipers pushes white clots across the glass, swishes them from side to side until they go transparent.

That last time. Devlan came to lunch. I cooked him lunch. And when he left I stood for perhaps half an hour with my back to the sink, watching the reflections from a bowl of water ripple on the ceiling. And then I felt light moving on my cheek, and it was the finches.

Light from a bowl of water in the sink, light rippling on the white ceiling. Light falling in a path across the floor, picking out a single orange in the fruit-bowl. The finches squabbling for peanuts, just at the window. The flakes of light that fell from their wings.

Devlan came in looking dowdy, crumpled, unshaven. He sat down heavily on a chair on the other side of the kitchen table and ran his hands over his face.

'I'm very tired,' he said. 'I nearly rang you to say I couldn't make it.'

I looked at him. I didn't answer.

'I had to run Rick to Gatwick this morning.'

'Early?'

'Yes.'

'Is he flying somewhere?' I said stupidly.

Devlan raised his head for a moment to look at me. 'Yes.'

'You could have cancelled.'

'Oh. Could I? I thought you . . .'

113

I turned and went to the stove. 'I've made some soup. I thought if I made a big batch it would last us all two days and you could have some,' I said.

'What sign are you?'

'I don't know.'

'What do you mean, you don't know?' Deborah raises her eyebrows.

'Well, Scorpio. I suppose I'm Scorpio.'

She is leafing through the free local paper. These days it is one of our favourite hobbies. 'You don't seem very sure.'

'Well, Scorpio or Libra. Sort of on the cusp.'

She's trying not to smile. 'I always thought you were a bit cuspy. So, which do you read?'

'Oh, both. Of course.' I try to sound emphatic. 'Or neither. If I'm reading them at all I always read both.'

'And which do you go by?'

'Oh, both. Or either. Whichever says things are getting better. I always believe anything that says things are getting better, don't you?'

'And which does say things are getting better?'

'Libra.' I grin back. 'Or Scorpio. Scorpio usually. There's that wonderfully expressive symbol. That barb in the tail tends to inspire confidence, don't you find?'

She snorts. 'Not when you're on the receiving end. Not when you suddenly find it inside your shoe!'

We both know it is the last time. 'Where shall we meet?' I ask Matthew. 'You suggest somewhere, and I'll join you. Better make it somewhere really ordinary. Then I won't have to dress up.'

His voice is tight as he answers me. 'No. You come here. We can eat here.'

'With Rex and Sheila?'

'They've gone away for the weekend. They've gone to see some friends of theirs in Hampshire. So I'm on my own.'

114

In memory I can see the house, the clipped lawn, the kitchen full of steam. His window. 'All right,' I say. 'What time shall I arrive?'

When I get there the house is in darkness. I go round to the back and try the door. It swings open. I grope my way upstairs and into what must be his bedroom. 'Matthew?' It comes out in an odd voice, something between a croak and a whisper. I feel for the light switch and turn on the light. His room is empty.

I go downstairs again and open the doors one by one. A neat square dining-room with Ercol chairs and a sideboard. A lounge with a low modern suite covered in a dark-red plush fabric. The hall itself with its mushroom-coloured paper on the walls and its venetian blinds. A view into a similar window in the yellow brickwork of the house next door, with its token straggle of creeper. Someone is standing there, talking into a telephone.

'Matthew?' I say again. Then I smell smoke. I push open the last door, the door of his parents' bedroom. He is sitting on the bed. The lighted end of his cigarette glows in the dark.

For a moment I can see nothing. Then he reaches out and turns on a lamp clipped to the headboard. It is angled away from him, casting its small pool of light downwards on to the carpet. But it is enough to see him by.

'Come here.' He has stubbed out the cigarette. The room is full of an odd smell which the smoke doesn't quite manage to disguise.

'Do you think I should?'

'Why not?'

'I came to say goodbye.'

'I know you did.'

'Can I say goodbye to you like this?'

'What other way is there?'

He takes hold of one of my hands and bends it back at the wrist, as far as it will go without breaking. I hear the bones crack. In the wardrobe mirror I can see my own face, not

115

moving. I am in my oldest, most shapeless clothes. My hair is unwashed, twisted into a plait. In the foreground, on the bedside table, Sheila's spare glasses, in a battered mock snake-skin case, a tortoiseshell hairbrush lying on its back with a comb stuck between the bristles, fine grey hairs wrapping them both like a cobweb. 'Chinese burn time?' I say.

He doesn't answer. I can feel his breath all over my body, as if he had many mouths. I feel him undressing me slowly. I lie there without moving. I might be dead. Then I seem to feel myself enter him, flow into him, wrapped tightly in the beautiful wet envelope of his skin.

On that last Saturday evening I am the first to arrive. I walk slowly up the steps and cross the room to the bar. 'Dry white wine, please, Charlie.' I get out my purse. 'Would you like something yourself?'

Over our heads the faded hops are dustier than ever. Only one of the fibre bells is still intact, its clapper still in place. But twined around and among them are garlands, colourful affairs studded with silk poinsettias and clusters of metallic berries. 'You've put in a lot of work on the decorations,' I say.

'Yeah. It's good for business. Atmosphere.' He screws up his eyes to see the white line just below the rim of the glass. 'They've all been telling me.'

I take a long mouthful. 'Did you see Matthew?'

'Not yet.'

I go over to the usual table, by the window. Just under me is a net of bare branches, threaded with little yellow lights. I wait ten minutes, twenty. I finish my wine and go to the bar again to buy another. When I turn to go back to my seat there is a pile of books on the table.

I turn to Charlie. 'Where did those come from?'

'Sorry?'

'The books. On the table. How did they get there?'

He shrugs. 'I haven't the faintest idea. I noticed them there just a moment ago. I assumed they were yours.'

'They *are* mine.'

'Did you lend them to someone?'

I don't answer him. I go to the window and look down. But below me the pavements are packed with late shoppers. Impossible in that crowd to pick out a single familiar head, even a red one. I open the book on the top of the pile. Inside the front cover he has stuck a Post-it. 'Sorry,' it says. 'I know what you're going to say, and I don't want to be there to hear it. Have a good Christmas.'

I shut myself in my bedroom. I draw the curtains across so that I don't have to look out on those trees. It is cold and grey, anyway. Even at midday there is hardly enough light to read or see your own face by. Annie is concerned. But she leaves me alone. When I emerge occasionally to make myself a drink or go to the bathroom, she hears my footsteps and runs to me and puts her arms round me. 'Mum. Are you all right?'

'Of course I am.' I hug her and retreat. 'I just don't feel very much like talking to anyone, okay?'

She goes downstairs again, her hand sliding down the rail. At the bottom she looks back at me and smiles.

Several times I hear a knock at the door. I hear her answer it. The phone rings, and I hear her low voice talking earnestly into the mouthpiece. When she sees me standing in the door she covers it with her hand. Then, on the Wednesday morning, she comes up to my bedroom with a cup of tea and two pieces of toast. 'I've brought you your breakfast.'

'Oh. Thanks. Are you getting on all right, darling?'

She looks at me. She puts the flat of her thumb against her lower lip in that way she still has. 'Mum, I'm leaving today. You did remember?'

I swallow. 'Yes, darling. Of course you are.'

'Will you be all right?'

'Yes,' I say. 'Why not?'

She is chewing at a loose bit of skin at the base of her thumbnail. 'Are you sure?'

'Of course I am.' I wave my hand over the mess of bed-clothes and letters and dirty plates. 'This will be all cleared up by the time you're halfway to Dover.'

'Only I do have to go. You know I have to go.'

I smile. 'Darling, honestly, it's only flu, or something. I'll be fine.'

'Actually . . .' Now she is picking at a piece of loose cotton in the weave of the bedspread. 'I'm all ready. I've got someone picking me up in half an hour.'

It's too dark in here to see her face properly. 'Give me one last hug, before you go,' I tell her. 'And take care of yourself.'

'And you.'

'Yes. I will. I promise I will.'

She collects up cups and glasses and bowls, and then she is gone. I hear her making a phone-call. I can't hear what she is saying. Then a car draws up outside and the house shakes as she slams the front door.

Later there is a loud knock. I go to answer it. It is Deborah. 'Let me in, Jan,' she says.

I step aside and let her come past me. She looks round her to left and right, but says nothing. She looks at me in my grease-spotted sweatshirt and torn canvas shoes. 'How are you?' she asks me.

'I'm okay. I've had some kind of bug. Flu or something. But I'm just about recovering.'

She frowns.

'Annie left this morning,' I tell her.

'I know. She phoned me to say she was leaving.' Deborah sits down at the table. I start working around her, clearing my mess of crumbs and coffee mugs, putting away the things from the draining-board. She doesn't offer to help me. She is reading the newspaper. She hardly seems to notice even that I am there. Finally I sit down with her. Outside it is beginning to get dark already, the grass losing whatever colour it had. I strain to read upside down, but in this light it is impossible. I reach up and flick the switch. 'How about this?' she says.

'What?'

She clears her throat.

' "Stuffed barn owls, pair, no question of splitting, immaculate, offers in region of £600.' "

'I haven't got £600.'

'Pity.'

'And I'm not keen on things that come in pairs.'

She makes a face. 'Well, what about this, then? "Page Boy Outfit, suit 7-year-old, olive-green trousers, cream shirt, mushroom satin waistcoat with matching bow tie, £25"?'

'We'd need a dummy to go with it.'

'We might be able to get hold of one from somewhere.' Then she sits up suddenly in her chair. When she speaks again there is real excitement in her voice. 'No. Wait. Listen. This one – "Wine bottle holder, wrought iron, reminiscent large birdcage, 4ft 6in tall, distinctive feature, £300." "Reminiscent large birdcage", isn't that lovely? "Distinctive feature." Don't you like the sound of that?'

'I haven't got £300.'

'Rubbish. And anyway I can lend you some. Haven't you always wanted a wine bottle holder that looked like a birdcage? Or a birdcage that looked like a wine bottle holder?'

' "O for a beaker full of the warm South," ' I say.

Her chair scrapes on the tiled floor. She stands above me, jingling her car-keys in her pocket. Then she goes to the phone.

I scarcely know where we are going. I am slumped in my seat, the branches passing over me like branches seen from the bottom of a boat, or from a pram. I feel slightly sick. Ahead of us her headlights are on full beam, searching the dark hedges. Once I sit up briefly and see a pair of gold eyes almost at ground level. They light up as we pass, then disappear into the dark. 'Did you see that?' I ask her.

Then we are arriving. I get out of the car and fill my lungs with the damp cold. We are at the centre of a modern housing estate: neat lawns, wheelie bins hiding in ornamental brick-work, cars parked on drives. I look up at the house. It could almost be Matthew's.

But the woman who answers the door has short fair hair, bleached into streaks. She peers at us from the lighted doorway. 'We rang, half an hour ago,' Deborah says. 'We've come to see the birdcage.'

'The wine bottle holder. Yes, of course. Come in. It's in the back.' We follow her into the hallway. Prints of flowers and birds wink at us under glass in shades of grey, beige, violet, blending with the mauve carpet. A cat comes out of the shadows and coils itself round my ankles. I bend down and scratch it under its chin and it closes its eyes. 'It's my father's, actually,' the woman is saying. 'He picked it up from some-where, on his travels. We've had it valued. I don't think you'll be disappointed.'

And we are not disappointed. A baroque bell-shaped trellis almost five feet high encloses emptiness. Parallel rows of wrought-iron smiles grow upwards from the base. 'That's where you put the bottles.' The woman reaches through the bars and touches the bent ironwork. It is slightly rusty. She rubs her finger against the side of her skirt. 'To stop them falling against one another and getting broken. I don't know how many it takes. We've never really counted.' The base itself is lined with a piece of old rag, threadbare velvet that must have been plum coloured, faded now to something closer to orange.

Deborah swallows. 'Three hundred pounds, you say?'

'Or near offer.'

Deborah and I look at each other. I raise my right hand and stroke the side of my nose.

'Two hundred and fifty?' Deborah gets out her cheque-book. The woman nods.

'Are you sure we'll get it into the car?' My voice sounds odd, higher than usual, almost a squawk.

'We'll have to.'

Between us we lift it gently. It is surprisingly heavy, for all its emptiness. Deborah is nearest the door. I push forward gently, steer us between the furniture. The top of the cage brushes the lampshade and for a moment the light swings madly, filling the room with drunken shadows. Then we are through the door and into the hall.

Next to the front door there is another door we haven't noticed. Now it is open. A bearded old man stands in the doorway, supporting himself on the doorframe. His hands are lumpy with arthritis. We lower the cage a few inches to get it through the front door and out on to the path. At the gate Deborah's car is waiting. 'Thanks,' I call to the woman, over my shoulder. 'We'll try and give it a good home.'

'I hope so.'

I glance back at her, trying to work out whether or not she is serious. But all I see is the old man, still gripping the doorframe as if he is afraid of falling, his mouth open, his tortoise eyes wet with tears.

When we get back we arrange the wine bottle holder in the place I have chosen for it, on a low table at the little side window. I open a bottle of wine. We sit back in our chairs and admire it, as the warmth comes to our faces. Deborah sighs. 'You know, it looks really good there.' She twists her glass. 'Really classy. But I'm just wondering if it wouldn't look even better on the middle landing.'

'What? Next to the laundry basket?'

'No, not there, you fool! I mean at the other end, by the telephone. Where you used to have that plant thing.'

'Would it fit in there?' I try to visualise it. 'Are you sure there'd be enough room?'

'At an artistic angle.' She is trying not to laugh. 'Leaning against the wall. You could display your collection of porcelain thimbles on those curly bits.'

'Oh. Right.' I take another swig of the wine.

There is a long silence. Then she says, 'It looks a bit empty.'

'It *is* empty. That's the point. Plenty of room for wine bottles. Or birds.'

'We should put something in it.'

'Like what?'

'Oh, I don't know . . . A candle?'

I get up and go to a drawer of the bureau. I take out a stub of candle. It is lopsided, one side bearded with congealed drips. I use a match to soften the wax and stick it upright on an old saucer. I open the little side-hatch of the cage and slide it in. Then I stretch out to touch the wick into flame. 'There. Satisfied?'

'Do you know what we should do?'

'No. What?'

'Have some sort of ceremony. Welcome it somehow.'

'You're joking!'

'Yes. Of course I am.'

But something makes me put down my glass and stand up. I feel unsteady. I must have drunk too much, or too quickly. But I put on a tape and start to dance. It is some ethnic band, Greek or Israeli, something Simon brought back from a trip once, a gift someone had given him in exchange for something. Deborah is laughing. It doesn't matter. She watches me, still grinning, as my skirt dips and swirls to the harsh melody. I have taken my shoes off. She is swaying now, in a parody of my movements. I laugh back at her and pull the elastic from my hair.

Then she stands up and joins me. We hold hands, bowing and turning slowly round the iron birdcage, raising our arms over it like witches. We pause to pick up our glasses. We stare at each other, out of breath. Then, still laughing, we flop down side by side on the carpet.

After a while I sit up and smooth my skirt over my knees. Our hands, flat on the carpet, are almost touching. Something about the wrought-iron circles is still making me feel dizzy. The light falls on them, silvering the outside edges of the curves, showing up the scabs where the metal has corroded. Then something falls on the table-top in front of me. I look at it, and it is gone. Another black speck has appeared six inches to its left. 'What's that?' I say.

Deborah has turned her empty glass upside down. The speck jumps and quivers inside it. 'Oh, God.'

'What?'

'That stupid cat. Why did you have to start stroking their fucking cat?'

'It's therapeutic,' Devlan said. 'You must keep on with it.'

'I'm not interested in therapy,' I told him. 'I just want it to be itself. I want what I write to stand on its own, somehow – outside me – for it to lay down terms in a way I never can.'

He smiled slightly, shuffling the sheets of paper against the steering-wheel. 'But all this is so personal. You haven't even . . .'

'You mean it's not art,' I said.

'Oh, "Art" . . .' He grimaced. 'That's always been a pretext for some of the most self-indulgent crap imaginable.'

I looked at him. My whole face was burning. 'If it's imaginable, then I'm going to let myself imagine it,' I said.

'You look happy!' Devlan leaned over to open the door on my side. 'What have you been up to?'

'I am happy. I went away for the weekend.'

'Oh? Where?'

'On a course. About writing stories.'

He drew out into the stream of traffic heading north. It was dusk already. The car-lights left luminous streaks of red and gold across my brain like a night photograph.

'And was it good?'

'Oh . . .' Ahead of us the shop-fronts parted, became trees. 'It was marvellous. The tutor was brilliant. And she actually liked some of my stuff! Do you know what she said to me?'

Devlan's face was impassive, his eyes on the road. 'And what were they like?'

'They?'

'The other students. You were in a group, surely?'

'Oh, yes. Of course. They were great too. I made friends with this really interesting woman who – '

'A lot of sharing took place.'

'I'm sorry?'

Devlan took his eyes from the road for a moment to smile at me. 'It was a T-group,' he said. 'That was a T-group you went to. Wonderfully cathartic. You can't tell me anything about those.'

I try to think back to that first film we saw together. I can still feel him in the dark beside me, watching the dance of those female bodies. I can still hear his breathing.

And there was something else, something I have almost allowed myself to forget. When he had talked about the woman with the socks, the one with the pills lined up on the bedside table, and I had wanted to laugh.

I didn't laugh. In fact I didn't feel remotely like laughing. Even the socks were horribly serious. I would feel them on my feet at odd moments, in the kitchen, or in bed at night, like the socks those childbirth manuals told you to wear for labour, thick and comforting and incongruous. And what I actually said was, 'Well, that's something you won't ever get from me.'

'What do you mean?'

I was angry. 'You won't get me trying to kill myself on your account!' I was angry. I was so angry I said it quietly, almost gently, as if it were some gift I were giving him.

'Oh. Good.' He shrugged. 'That's all right, then.'

> Yet love I must or else I die.
> Or else I die, I die.

*

124

What happened? Nothing. No money changed hands. We argued. And I lost. *But I haven't got hundreds of thousands of pounds. I haven't even got a hundred. I've only got a husband and children, and half a house.* And ever since then the other half has been full of whispers.

We say goodbye, not in the café or at Perry's or in his parents' bedroom. There is nowhere we can possibly say goodbye to each other but by the river. We are walking. It is suddenly cold. A frost has baked the mud into hard ridges under our feet. We both have our hands in our pockets. We hardly look at each other.

We reach the clearing where I told him about Simon. We lean side by side against an overhanging branch. It is willow, springy. It gives slightly under us and bounces almost on the water. A few last long leaves brush the surface and shake free again, sparkling.

I steal a look at his profile.

He looks back at me. He is pale. The summer freckles have faded.

'Well? Which one of us is going to be the one to say it?' I hear myself ask him.

He is looking away from me now, towards the opposite bank. 'I don't know. You're the one with all the experience. You tell me.'

Matthew is the one to say it. We are in the Hole in the Wall, squashed together on a bench near the door. Around us students bang down their glasses, lean towards one another, laughing at a shared joke, jogging our elbows. Someone stands up to go to the bar and stumbles against Matthew's knee, making him slop his beer on the table. Over our heads the outsize red metallic snowflakes shiver in the updraught. 'It's time we stopped seeing each other,' he says.

I count ten before replying. Then I say, carefully, 'I've got something for you.'

'A goodbye present?'

'You could say that.' I get a small parcel out of my pocket and put it on the table in front of him. I have wrapped it in kitchen towel, white with a seasonal pattern of poinsettias and holly. I have been carrying it round with me for some weeks.

'What is it?'

'Open it and see.'

He picks it up by one corner and it unwraps itself, unravelling in the air until the key falls out and hits the wood of the table with a crack. 'A key?' He stares at me. 'What is this?'

'It's the key to the shop,' I tell him.

'But we . . . I just told you, I'm not going to see you any more.'

'Exactly.'

'And you want to give me your key?'

'It's to the shop. Just a gesture. You can come in there when you like, when I'm not around. You can turn off the alarm and just go in there and browse. You can unlock the till and buy anything that takes your fancy. You can even steal something, if you want to. I won't mind.'

'But I don't see the point . . .'

'You're the only other person to have one,' I tell him. 'Apart from Oliver.'

'But I really don't . . .'

I reach for his hand and pull it towards me across the table-top, as if I were going to read his palm. I close his fingers over the key gently, one by one. 'Take it, Matthew. You never know. Just take it.'

'Have you got any brothers and sisters?' I asked Devlan once.

'One brother,' he said. 'No sisters.'

'Older than you, or younger?'

'Younger.'

'Do you get on?'

'When we see each other.'

126

'Does he live a long way away, then?'

'Not really. In the Midlands somewhere. He's married. Three children.'

There was something odd about him as he said it, a tightness I seemed to recognise. 'Don't you get on with his wife?'

'Oh, Melissa's been the making of him. She's a strong woman. A strong woman.' He laughed and shook his head. 'Better than a sister to me. And without all the usual disadvantages.'

There was a silence. 'Wouldn't you have wanted a sister?' I asked him.

'No.'

'Why not?'

'Why do you think?'

'Because she would have understood you?'

Devlan smiled slightly. 'Because she would have been a cow,' he said.

Once I actually caught him out. 'That's the very opposite of what you told me last week!' I was triumphant.

He raised his eyebrows. 'Really?'

'Yes. You're contradicting yourself completely. Last week you were saying . . .'

'And does it matter?'

'Does what matter?'

'That what I say isn't always the same thing? Why do you need me to be consistent?'

It was a catch question. I hesitated for a long time before answering.

Finally he said, 'Needing other people to behave consistently is an index of your own dependency. Are you aware of that?'

I heard myself take in my breath sharply with a kind of whistle, in that way he had. 'I shall be, from now on.'

And which of the many voices did he use? In my head I try them all for size, to remember. Was it the boyish voice?

The hard cool voice? The voice that was two tones lower? 'I don't think I know what you want of me,' he said.

'What do you want me to want of you?' I was sitting on the floor, my head almost against his knee.

'Something I can give you.'

'What can you give me?'

There was a long silence. The tears were running into my mouth. I shifted my position at his feet and reached up for his hand.

'This I can give you,' he said.

We walked back along the embankment, towards the place where he had parked the car. The wind tore at us, snatching at his raincoat and pulling it open. He walked with his hands in his pockets. Over my shoulder the river lights shivered. 'I lied to you,' I told him suddenly.

'Well...' He was striding on ahead, the wind tearing the words out of his mouth so I had to strain to hear them. I ran a few paces to keep up with him. 'That's your prerogative.'

'Devlan, wait.'

He turned round to face me, the wind flapping in his clothes, his fists like two weights in the pockets. I thought I saw him sigh. 'What did you lie to me about?'

'About my father.'

'Really.'

'When I said I hated him.'

'Ah.'

'You do remember?'

'I do remember,' Devlan said.

'And I was lying.' The wind caught my hair and blew it into my eyes, making them water. 'When I said I hated him. I was lying. I don't hate him at all.'

'Of course you don't.'

'I never have hated him.'

'Well. I'm glad about that.' I can hear him saying it now, finally. He stood there in front of me for a moment, rocking backwards and forwards on his heels. Then he turned and started to walk on.

The worst thing he ever said to me? It's hard to remember, there were so many worst things. But once, as we stood together in my basement kitchen, watching the feet go past. What was it he said?

I was trying not to look at him. On every surface the dirty cups and plates surrounded us. At any moment they could slide down on to the floor with a crash of breakage. But perhaps the impact would be broken by the piles of stale laundry that tangled under my feet. I sat down at the table and put my head in my hands. 'There's nothing, is there? Nothing you can say or do.' The tears were finding their way out between my fingers.

I heard him suck in his breath. It was almost a whistle. Then he said, 'Your poor family.'

And I stood up to face him. Then, very deliberately, I picked up Laura's half-eaten bowl of cereal and threw it at his head.

Even before he walked through the door I knew that was the last time. I was only waiting for some small acknowledgement. I finished the cheese on my plate and raised my glass to him. 'All in all, you treated me rather badly,' I said.

He picked up a last sliver of Stilton and balanced it on a biscuit, before putting it in his mouth. He savoured it. Then he said, 'Actually, I was rather nice to you.'

'Nice? What do you mean?' I pushed back my chair and stood up. I crossed the kitchen to where the coffee-maker was wheezing rhythmically. '*Nice?*'

'Yes. Nice.' The words echoed. 'I could have taken advantage of you.'

'But I never . . .' My voice was starting to shake. I went out into the hall and took his shapeless old coat down from its hanger. He came and took it from me without a word.

*

For a long time I stood with my back to the kitchen sink, watching the reflections on the ceiling. I was so still that after a while the greenfinches came. Inches from my eyes, on the other side of the glass, they fought over the peanuts, their racing wings a blur against the light. As they fought, I could feel the wing-shadows cutting my cheek, just under my right eye.

We are standing in the sitting-room, I on one side, towards the kitchen, and Matthew still almost in the doorway, as if ready to leave. It is damp and grey outside, rain dripping along the bare branches, running down under the eaves, filling the water-butt with a rich gurgle. And all over Europe it is the same or worse. Only last night I saw it on the news – the centre of Cologne under water, boats in the streets. And in Holland hundreds of thousands of people forced to evacuate their homes. The water on both sides of the dike rising, divers shoring up the vulnerable places with sandbags. And one old man was still living upstairs in his own house, on a diet of goodness knows what. He stood at his window and shouted at the rescue people. 'Why should I leave? What should I leave *for*? I've got everything I need.' I turn the electric light on and see it light up Matthew's hair.

'I've got something for you,' I tell him.

'Yes?'

'Here.' I go over to the desk and take the picture out of its translucent envelope. I hand it to him. 'Do you remember this?'

He shrugs almost imperceptibly. 'It's me. That first walk by the river. The scenery's incredible.'

'I had it enlarged. I thought you'd like to keep it. It's a very good one – of you, anyway.' I peer over his shoulder. Under the astonishing fringe he is smiling at the camera. There is a leaf in his hair.

He smiles now as he looks at me and pushes his glasses

higher. His voice is heavy with sarcasm when he says, 'Is this goodbye?'

'Not necessarily. That's entirely up to you.'

'You mean, if I behave myself . . .'

I am smiling too.

'I don't want it.' He gives it back to me. His glossy face bends and flashes under the light.

'No. I didn't think you would.' I am still smiling as I tear the photograph into small pieces and throw it into the grate.

We were holding hands. I couldn't even look at him. My voice was unrecognisable, the lowest it had ever been. 'If I were you, I would be *ashamed*.' And he shrugged. I can't even remember what he said.

CHAPTER 7

WEDDING DRESS, IVORY satin, size 10, full length with short train, bodice embroidered lilies of the valley, unworn, cost £300. Quick sale £70.

BATMAN LOOKING for Robin to service Batmobile. Mechanical skills an advantage.

ANDY PANDY calling for Looby Loo/ Teddy. Let me pull your strings! Time to go home to a wall of daisies.

COUNTERFEIT DETECTOR PENS, imported, will detect forged notes (British and most international currencies) with speed and proven accuracy. Bulk orders welcome.

MALE WANTS female, any age, to slake unslakable lust. Looks irrelevant. Soh a liability.

DENTIST'S CHAIR, 1950's model, leather, offers.

Il bianco e dolce cigno cantando more,
Ed io piangendo giung'al fin del viver mio.
Stran'e diversa sorte,
Ch'ei more sconsolato,
Ed io moro beato.

I am at the kitchen sink, still washing up the breakfast things. I have turned on the radio for company. I reach down into the soapsuds. A male voice says, 'And this has been requested by Emma, for Matthew. I hope you're listening, Matthew?' I drop the mug I am holding back into the water. The front of my sweatshirt is covered with splashes. I hardly hear the music. At the end of it I have no idea what they have been playing. I look up out of my window on a bank of heavy cloud. From its lower edge shafts of sunlight stream to earth, picking out the clump of Scots pines on the top of the hill.

Finally, in the late afternoon, I slip out. I tell myself it is to buy cigarettes, though I still have two left, more than enough. For a moment I wonder whether to stop at a phone-box and ring Deborah. But she will think I am mad, even madder than usual. She will say, 'But why are you ringing from a call-box? What's wrong with your phone at home?' And I shall have to explain it. I start walking vaguely in the direction of the village. It's then that I meet the woman.

She is wearing trousers and a shapeless anorak. She accosts me almost aggressively. 'Is there an off-licence somewhere here? They told me there was an off-licence.'

I tell her there is. 'I don't know if it's open, though.'

'Is there a pub?'

I tell her there is a pub up on the left. I have just come past it. It was in darkness and obviously closed. There is another one almost opposite, but that's probably shut as well.

I walk up past the off-licence. It is closed. I go as far as the garage. That's shut too. The signs aren't illuminated. So I come back.

I pass her again. She is still wandering. 'I haven't been any luckier than you,' I tell her.

This time she is even more aggressive. 'Is there a pub near here?'

'Yes,' I say. 'There are two pubs. They're both shut.'

'Where are they?' She doesn't seem to believe me.

I don't know why, I get hold of her gently by the shoulders and turn her round so she is facing the pub. 'There,' I say. 'Just opposite. The Spanner in the Works. It's shut.'

She mutters something. She is angry. 'What's the time?'

'Well,' I say. 'It *is* Christmas Day . . .'

'*What's the time?*' she shouts at me.

'*I don't know!*' I say. I roll up my sleeve so she can see my wrist. '*I haven't got a watch.*'

When I get back the phone is ringing. I struggle with my key in the dark. At first it doesn't seem to fit the keyhole. On the other side of the door I can hear the double rings of the bell, still continuing. Then the key slides into the lock and I turn it. The door swings open. I run through to the kitchen and pick up the receiver.

It is Rex. At first I don't recognise the voice. Then he says gruffly, 'Mrs Hickman? This is Rex Donaldson. I was just wondering if Matthew was there with you? I'm so sorry to disturb you at a family time like this.'

'It doesn't matter.' I am still gasping from my efforts with the door. 'Matthew? No. Why would he be here?'

'Well . . .' I have embarrassed him. 'I did understand that you and he . . .'

'Oh, well, yes. But not now. Not over Christmas,' I say quickly. 'I assumed he was living it up with you.'

'We usually take life very quietly, Mrs Hickman.' He sounds strange. He isn't reacting. He coughs. 'To tell you the truth, we're a bit worried, his mother, especially. Well, obviously he's a grown man, and what he chooses to do and who he chooses to see is his own business. We've always tried to be aware of that. It's not easy, you know, having him here at home, without making him feel ... But we've done our best. And he does usually let us know if he's going to be away for a few days, for interviews and so forth.'

'*A few days?*'

'Well, yes. He walked out of here two days ago, and we haven't seen hide nor hair of him since.'

'And you don't know where he is?' My mind fixes on an image, a face lit up in the glow from my brake-lights as I reverse.

'We were hoping ... Sheila was hoping he might be with you.'

'I'm sorry. I haven't seen him.'

'Oh, well ...' Rex gives a strained laugh. 'He's a big boy now. He can look after himself. I shouldn't worry. The last thing I wanted to do was to worry you.'

'Thank you.' *And stop worrying yourselves. You're good parents. Sheila's been a good mother. I can tell, I ... It's me. It's my fault. I made him ...* 'Thank you,' I say to him again. 'He must just have gone to stay with someone else. As you say, he's old enough to look after himself. You mustn't worry.' I put down the phone and lean against the wall. Around me the remains of my Christmas dinner are still strewn across every surface. The miniature turkey joint, a last crumbling fragment of the individual pudding, the Brussels sprouts gone soft and slimy, stray dark leaves sticking to the sides of the colander. My own plates and cutlery. I go to the bottom of the stairs and call Annie. 'Are you there, darling? Would you like to help with the washing-up?' Then I remember she has gone.

'There's no need at all in this world for punishment,' Devlan said to me once. 'Why punish a child when you can get it to do what you want by other means?'

'Like bribery?' I said.

He gave a short laugh. 'In management terminology it's called "positive reinforcement".'

'Meaning?'

'Meaning that when someone who works for you does something you want to encourage, you encourage it.'

'How?'

'You give them a reward.'

'Like luncheon vouchers?'

He smiled. 'You don't like this idea much, do you?'

'No,' I said. 'I think it's patronising. I think it's manipulative. It stinks.'

He shrugged. 'Well, you don't have to take it on board. If punishment is more your bag.'

'Like what, then? What kind of reward?'

'Like status. Like their own telephone line. Or a bigger office. Like a key.'

'A *key*?'

'To the main entrance, or the safe. Whatever.'

'And do you give all your friends keys, to reward appropriate behaviour?'

'Sure.' He laughed. He jingled something in his pocket. 'Here you are. I had this cut this morning especially for you.'

'What is it?'

'It's a key.'

'But what does it unlock?'

'Nothing,' he said. 'Aren't those the kind you like best?'

All over Europe the floods are rising. Ancient German cities succumb one by one, their cellars awash with sewage. In France mobile homes are washed down river to find themselves half suspended in trees, their bedding soaked through with brown water, crockery sliding from the shelves. In Holland an old man refuses to be moved. Outside his window the boats come and go. Public servants address him with loud-hailers, and he greets them with obscene gestures. A woman who once loved him stands up and gesticulates frantically to catch his attention, making the boat rock.

Matthew is walking down by the river, in darkness. His red hair has gone dark with the rain, plastered to his forehead. His glasses are misted over, so that he can hardly see. He crosses the old bridge, as far as its centre. He stands only a few feet over the rushing water, where it drags at the masonry, well above its usual dark line. The semi-circle of stones has shrunk to a small arc. The graduated post with its painted warning is almost completely submerged.

And I write him a letter. On my knees I write him a letter. *Matthew, Debbie's having a few people round for New Year's Eve. Will you come? Forgive me. Please come. Love, Jan. Please. Love. I'm sorry.* I pick up the pen and write, 'Dear Matthew.' He leans over the parapet and looks down. He seems to be trailing one hand in the water.

Sometimes in shell the orient pearls we find.

And perhaps the solution was always just to write. Writing specialises in unfinished business. But how to catch the voices – the hard voice you could crack an egg on, the boy's forgotten voice, the problematic voice that sank ever lower? And my own, asking the questions.

It is easier to pick up the long shreds of Simon's shirt and tie them together into a rope that will reach to the front gate, and beyond.

It is easier to arrange the rope itself into words across the floor. 'Your poor family,' it says, in fraying cursive. Or 'my poor family'. I sit down in the centre of one of the o's and see the writing stretch away from me in every direction, a sea of torn white waves. And I think of poor families, of thousands and thousands of poor families everywhere, the white knots just holding them together. The white rope that will let them escape from their burning houses. The way they stand shivering in the rain, with no shirt to cover their backs.

Gsoh. After Devlan, I had applied for that job. I was exhausted. Laura and Annie had just had chicken-pox. Devlan had offered to write me a reference. When I got a copy of the letter he had written, it was full of compliments in his usual idiom. It reminded me of a letter from someone writing in a foreign language.

The job was for a women's organisation in London. It was way out of my reach. When I got through to the last round of interviews I put it down to Devlan's reference.

On the day of the final interview I had a pain in my left shoulder. At first it was only an ache. Then it was worse. My whole back and left arm were throbbing. I could hardly concentrate on the questions the panel put to me. I must have been squirming in my chair. 'Are you all right?' the president asked me, almost aggressively. 'You look uncomfortable. Why do you keep wriggling about in your chair?'

It didn't occur to me to lie. 'I'm sorry. I'm in pain,' I said.

'Oh, dear. Do you suffer from back problems?'

'No. Not usually. I'm so sorry.'

She pursed her lips and looked down. I saw her turn over a sheet of paper on her desk. Then she stood up and held out her hand. The room heaved as I pushed back my chair and straightened my spine.

When I got home I went straight to bed. I couldn't lie still. The pain was making me sick. I went down to the bathroom and vomited into the flat water of the toilet. I was shaking. Then I turned round. Simon was standing behind me in the open doorway. 'I feel terrible. Do you think you could ring the doctor?' I said. 'I think I need help.'

'What do you want me to say?'

'I don't know.' My teeth were chattering. The back of my

nose was clogged with sick. 'I don't know.' I steadied myself on the doorframe as the pain surged back.

I dragged myself upstairs and rolled in between the covers. I tried to breathe deeply. Downstairs I could hear Simon's low voice on the telephone.

Then he was standing by the bed. I opened my eyes. 'Did you ring?'

He nodded.

'What did he say?'

'He said to try and drink something. No solids, he said.'

'Is that all?'

'He asked if you'd been under any special strain lately.'

I heard myself make an odd sound.

'I told him I didn't think there had been anything unusual.'

I shouldn't be doing this. I am too tired. I am too old. *Don't let your foot hang off the back of the step. You'll be asking for tendon trouble.* My foot slips on the rubber surface and I almost lose my balance.

But I go on. Something makes me go on, the music or the other women with their blank faces, or my own face frozen in an empty smile. By the end of every session my fingers are swollen. Once I lose the feeling in my left foot and have to stamp it back to life, like a child who has been kneeling too long on the floor. Occasionally my eyes are bloodshot. But it is clean. We hardly even say hello to one another. I tell myself it would be a good way to go.

'Devlan.' I say the name and wait for the shock, the shame and disgust I am so familiar with. At first, nothing. And then a light tingling like disbelief. Somewhere an extremity still twitches, a nerve aches, a dream still struggles to run against the current. But it isn't what it was.

Ten years on, fifteen, twenty years on, and the statistics are shown to be in error. My life is not what it was. Matthew pushes back his wet hair and gets out a cigarette, struggles to light it in the rain. The paper is wet, spotted with the grey splashes of raindrops. *And Devlan is an old man now.* Ten years by ten years a life changes, until the statistics are finally silenced. Until in the end there is no possible room left for doubt.

Three days after Christmas Deborah comes to see me. From the kitchen I see her outline through the frosted glass. Then she goes round to the front and pounds on the door with all her strength until I get up and go to answer it.

'Why didn't you let me in?'

'I didn't hear you.'

'Don't be ridiculous! I could see you sitting there. Why did you have to make me beat the door down?'

'I haven't got anything to say to anyone.'

'Too bad,' she says. She is carrying a small bunch of flowers, winter jasmine and snowdrops, a first spray of pussy willow. She fills a vase with water and starts to stick them into it haphazardly. 'But I've got something to say to you.'

I get up to go into the other room. She is still talking, but from here it isn't quite so loud.

But she has followed me. 'Do you realise I've had Matthew at my house for two days?'

'Well, that's a relief. Rex and Sheila must have been almost beside themselves. I hope he said "Thank you for having me".'

'Jan.' Deborah's voice is very serious. 'He really was in a bad state. I just put him up for a couple of nights, while he got himself together. I didn't say anything. But when I hung up his coat a full bottle of sleeping-pills fell out of his pocket.'

'We all have difficulty sleeping sometimes. We all have unfinished business, we're all . . .'

'Stop it, Jan,' Deborah says. 'What the fuck do you think you're *doing*?'

'I'm not doing anything!'

'Yes, you are. You're winding him up somehow. You've got some sort of sinister axe to grind. I *know* you!'

'I love him,' I tell her.

'What difference does that make?'

'A lot. It makes all the difference.'

'It makes it easier. You know where to get him, what strings to pull.'

'I'm not pulling any strings.'

'I don't believe you.'

There is a silence. In the kitchen a tap is dripping. We both look at our feet.

When Deborah speaks again her voice is gentler, almost affectionate. But the exasperation is still there. 'And what did you tell him about Simon, for God's sake?'

'I don't know. I don't remember. Why? What did you tell him?'

She looks at me. 'I told him the *truth*!'

The next morning the post falls on to my door-mat with a soft thump. I pick it up and take it through to the kitchen. I turn the letters over one by one in my hand before I open them. Gas estimate, bank statement, a few late cards. I open them, one by one. *From Simon, Leah, Josh and Chloe, with love.* And one that is lumpy, heavier than the others.

I open it. There is a piece of folded kitchen towel inside, plain white. I undo it gently, as if I expected it to hold something valuable.

But there is only the key, and a short note, folded into a small square. I have hardly seen enough of Matthew's handwriting to be sure even that it is his.

'Sorry. I'm returning this. I did try it, actually, and it didn't work. The cutting must have been faulty. You'll have to get them to redo it if you need it for someone else.'

Five days after Christmas, I get a call from Deborah. Her voice is strange, precarious. I can hear a kind of tightness in her throat, as if she is trying to swallow something. 'What is it? What's the matter?' I ask her.

'Oh, Jan. Nothing.' I wait, but she only repeats it. 'Nothing.' Then her voice breaks. 'Nothing I can put my finger on.'

'What is it?'

'I don't know.'

'Where are you?'

'Here. At home.'

'Is anyone there with you?'

'No.'

'Hang on,' I tell her. 'I'm coming.'

When I get there her house is in darkness. I go round to the back door and push. It isn't locked. I turn on the light. Her kitchen is icy. I can see my breath. I go into the front room. She is sitting on the floor in the dark, her head resting on the seat of a chair. 'Deb?' I say.

She looks up at me and half smiles.

'What's wrong?'

'Nothing. I told you. Nothing I can put my finger on. I'm ashamed of myself. But thanks.'

'Is it Sean? The other day you seemed so happy.'

'I *am* happy.'

'It looks like it!'

'No, really . . .' She struggles to get up and I put my hand on her shoulder.

'It's all right. Stay there. Let's try and warm ourselves up a bit. It's like an igloo in here!'

I go out into the kitchen and start rummaging through the cupboards. I find some packets of instant soup and put on a kettle. I carry hers in to her in a mug.

She sits up straight and holds it between her two hands. 'This is so stupid!'

'Don't say anything.' I am rolling small balls out of news-paper from the store she keeps on a shelf to one side of the hearth. Then I put twigs in on top of it, built into a neat wigwam. I strike a match. As the flames catch and spread I start to feed them with wood, first the finest pieces, almost like splinters, and then the bigger chunks. The fire sparks and splutters. The split logs begin to hiss. It is almost ready for the coal now. I turn to her. She is hunched on the rug with a blanket round her shoulders. The tears run down her face steadily, into her mouth.

'It's okay,' I say. 'It doesn't matter. None of it matters.'

'You sound like my mother.'

'Yes. Well.' She moves closer to me and lays her head in my lap. I can smell the scent of her hair. My hand is stroking the top of her head. 'Did you hear about the two women?' I ask her.

'What two women?'

'The ones on the mountain. The ones they'd almost given up hope for.'

'Did they find them?'

'Yes. They found them. And they were all right. They'd had the gumption to dig themselves into a snow-hole and sit out the blizzard. And when the blizzard lifted, they found them. And they were fine.'

'They survived.'

'Unscathed.'

For a long time we sit there, watching the fire. I am remembering the fires of my childhood, the way my father roasted chestnuts. After a while my legs go numb. I move them, cautiously. I can tell from Deborah's breathing that she is asleep.

Late that night the phone rings. Deborah? Or perhaps it is Annie, ringing to tell me she has got back safely. But when I pick up the receiver a man's voice is speaking. 'Mrs Hickman?' It sounds urgent.

'Yes?'

'You're the owner of the Castle Bookshop in the High Street?'

145

'Yes.' I don't have time to be frightened, only to hang on.

'I'm afraid there's been a fire.'

I am too surprised to say anything.

'Don't worry. It's not too serious. The fire service people are there already and everything's under control. There's minor damage. Nothing structural. Smoke, of course. And wet carpets. And a few of the books may have caught the brunt of it. You might like to get on to your insurance company first thing in the morning.'

'Should I come in?'

'Well . . .' He gives a short laugh. 'You can if you like. There isn't actually much you can do. We had to break in to gain access. And I believe a colleague of yours is already on the premises.'

'Oliver.'

'I'm sorry?'

'He lives almost next to the shop. He must have been there almost from the beginning.'

'That's the one. Well, as I say, you needn't . . .'

'I'll come in. Just give me half an hour, and I'll be with you.'

'It isn't necessary. Really.'

'What do you think I'm going to do, then? Go to bed and go straight to sleep?'

By the time I arrive there is no sign of flames anywhere. I had half expected gouts of orange fire roaring from the upstairs windows. But there isn't anything. Not even the hiss of water on hot masonry. The firemen have already packed up and gone. There is only a slight persistent bitter smell that isn't really even like smoke.

There is no need to open the front door. It swings open. My feet squelch over sodden carpeting. In the faint glow from the lights opposite I can pick out the gleam of water, charred paper, dark shadows on the walls. Somewhere near the back of the shop a small circle of light moves over the shelves. 'Oliver?'

The small white beam searches for me and finds me. Beyond it there is darkness. I blink, caught in it like a moth or a burglar. 'Can you shine that thing somewhere else?'

He points it downwards and I see an irregular white scrap of paper. I bend down and pick it up. It is almost triangular, two of its edges clean and untouched, and the other a longer jagged slash of charred black. 'Helen Quinnell has been involved in expl . . . of one form or another sin . . .' I crumple it in my hand and throw it back.

'It's not too bad, actually.' Oliver runs the torch along the top shelves to show me the rows of books, untouched. 'Not nearly as bad as it looks. And I suppose the insurance people will come through.'

'Oh, yes. Surely. But all the same it's going to be quite a lot of work.'

'How long do you think it'll take us?'

'Oh, not too long. Two days? What do you think? I'll have to close the shop while we clean up, of course.'

'Well, I'll be here tomorrow morning as usual, with my little mop and bucket.'

I pat him on the shoulder. 'Wear old clothes. I'll get on to the insurance people first thing. They'll want to see it before we start. Then you can help me choose the paint.' I have a sudden thought. 'I suppose the computer's all right, and the answering machine?'

'Oh, yes. I'm sure they are. Nothing in the back has been hurt at all. This is where it started. You can tell just by looking.'

There is a short silence. Then I say, 'How did it start? Have they any idea?'

'Electrical fault.' Oliver gives me a wry smile. 'At least, that's what they're saying.'

'No sign of any intentional damage?'

'Not as far as I could gather. Anyway, the firemen had to break the door to get in.'

'Yes.' I am smiling back at him. I take the torch from his hand and shine it at the ceiling. The lampshade dangles from

147

its flex in dark shreds. 'Of course they did. Come on.' I reach out and brush a flake of ash from his left shoulder. His earring glints at me. 'There's nothing we can do tonight. Let's go home.'

He follows me out, his feet squelching behind me on the sodden carpet. I wait for him. I reach into my pocket for the key.

But when I try to fit it into the lock, something is not quite right. The little noise it makes as it enters the keyhole is somehow different from usual. And when I go to turn it it resists me. *Matthew. The key I gave him.* I feel in my pocket again and my fingers come into contact with something else. This time the lock clicks to.

Once, about a year afterwards, he rang me. 'How are you?' It was the bland voice.

I was shaking. 'Fine,' I said. 'How are you?'

'Oh, fine.'

'How's business?' I'd heard rumours that he'd set up independently somewhere, offering courses in presentation skills and counselling. Psychotherapy too, I heard. 'How're the power and the authority these days?'

He laughed easily, as if it were a joke we shared. 'That's why I'm calling you, actually.'

'Oh?'

'We wondered if you might be interested in working for us.'

'Me?' I took a deep breath. Then I asked carefully, 'What sort of thing did you have in mind?'

'Oh . . . assertiveness, creative therapy, something like that. Something you could do on your head. We need to broaden our programme, particularly for the overseas market.'

'I'll think about it,' I said.

Then the gentler, younger voice. 'I thought you might like to have lunch and talk about it.' He sounded almost wistful.

I hesitated. The receiver in my hand had stopped jumping

about now. I could relax my jaw without thinking my teeth would start to chatter. 'I suppose I might,' I said.

'You've never been here before, have you? Let me show you round.' I climbed out of his car and followed him in through the Victorian doorway with its raised square pattern. Along a dark passage that smelled of damp stone. Then into a large bare expanse of polished sunlight. 'This is the main teaching room.' He pulled at the projector-screen and let it go to reveal a gleaming white-board behind. 'You can see, it's got all the usual facilities.'

I nodded without speaking. I followed him from room to room. 'This is the office,' he said.

I stumbled over the threshold and nearly tripped over a man. He was sitting cross-legged on the floor with the phone between his knees. 'Oh, I don't think you've ever met. This is my partner. Let me introduce you. Jan – Rick.' The man looked up at me, a cool look, not quite hostile. I looked back. 'You don't mind if Rick comes to lunch with us, do you?'

What I remember now is waiting for him in a side room, while the two of them got ready. I remember the lovely old windows, the sun that lit the parquet as if for dancing, the shrubs outside, clipped box and laurel that someone once had planted with something that had approximated to love.

I waited for ten minutes while they tied up loose ends. Then we were at a small country pub, the three of us. It was called the Golden Ball. The sign had a picture of a frog sitting on a lily-pad. 'What will you have? I can recommend the lasagne,' Devlan said.

'Fine,' I said. Somehow I found myself sitting facing the window. I had to squint to see their faces, side by side half blocking the light.

'Let me get us all some wine.' Rick stood up and went to the bar. In a moment he was back with a bottle and three glasses. He poured mine right to the rim, then Devlan's, then his own. For a fraction of a second their eyes met. Devlan turned to face me, his two hands flat on the table. He smiled. 'You can see the kind of framework we have here,' he said. 'So how do you think you might fit in?'

They took turns to question me, Rick leaning back in his chair, his hands joined behind the back of his head.

'May I know what you're offering me?' I could feel the anger creeping into my voice.

Neither of them answered. They exchanged glances. Then Devlan said, almost under his breath, 'Oh, by the way, as regards that other matter, I think we can forget it and move on to consider the alternatives, don't you?'

That other matter? Did he think I couldn't hear him? Did he think I couldn't see him as he leaned slightly sideways to say it? I could almost feel myself dissolving. A shaft of sunlight seemed to fall through my arm across the dark stained wood of the table, picking out a knife-blade. I stood up suddenly, my chair falling backwards and hitting the floor with a clatter. I pushed through towards the door and out into the clear autumn afternoon. I stood by the car, filling my lungs.

They were following me, their heads close together, laughing about something. Devlan unlocked the doors. He drove back fast the way we had come. 'You can handle all that?' he called out to Rick as he dropped him off.

'Oh, sure.' Rick leaned in through the window and stretched out his hand. 'It's been very interesting. I'm so glad to have met you.'

'Thank you.' I was still concentrating on my breathing. I ignored the hand. Whatever happened, I would keep my voice level. 'I hope the other little matter doesn't give you too much gyp.'

Devlan drove in silence. We hardly looked at each other. The fields and woods slipped past, the sheep clinging to the sides of the hills. The clouds were coming up now. A huge tree stood alone on a village green, the ground under it a perfect circle of leaves like rust. Then there was a panorama over my shoulder, to the east. He glanced at it. Then he glanced at me. He said quietly, 'How are you *really*, these days?'

I looked at him, his profile, his hands on the wheel. 'Oh, okay. Surviving. Yes . . .' I hesitated. 'Surviving. What about you?'

'Oh, all right. Fine, really, all things considered.'

'And the new venture?'

'Oh, yes. Excellent. At least . . .'

'Problems?'

'No. Not really. Nothing at all worrying. If only this wretched woman wouldn't keep writing to everyone on our mailing-list . . .'

I looked at him. 'What do you mean? What woman?'

He shrugged. 'Some woman. I don't know.'

I felt something inside me give a lurch. The thin floor of the car was rising and falling under my feet. My body felt suddenly crushable and absurd. 'What does she say to them?'

'Oh, nothing. What can she say to them?' He turned to me and grinned. 'That we're sharks, that we're incompetent, you know the kind of shit.'

I took a deep breath. I was beginning to understand what he was telling me. I hesitated. 'When did it start?'

'Oh . . .' He was trying to think back. 'A few months ago.'

'Do you know who it is?'

'Yes. I think so. Probably.'

We were coming down the hill now, into the town. Around us people were walking, carrying plastic bags of shopping. Devlan pulled up at a light. 'You know, I told Rick about you, how you would never be the kind of person to do anything remotely . . .'

'Why did you get me over, then? Why did you put me through all that? What a farce!' I swallowed. 'You know there was never anything between us. Nothing I could possibly feel angry about. I never even think of you these days.'

He looked at me mildly. 'You're wrong.' His voice had

151

suddenly gone serious. 'Actually I've always thought it was terribly important. For me, for you . . .'

'Not for me,' I said. 'Not now.'

> She never wanders far abroad,
> But is at home when I do call.
> If I command she lays on load
> With lips, with teeth, with tongue and all.
> She chants, she chirps, she makes such cheer,
> That I believe she hath no peer.
> For when she once hath felt a fit,
> Philip will cry still: yet, yet, yet, yet.
> For when she once hath felt a fit,
> Philip will cry still: yet, yet, yet, yet,
> Yet, yet, yet, yet, yet, yet,
> Yet, yet, yet, yet.

It is done now. It is finished. He discovered the coward in me, the child, the fool. And I am none of these things.

One day I shall meet him. It will be one summer when I am driving Annie and a friend of hers back from Heathrow. I leave the motorway to find the friend's address, somewhere in the suburbs near where he must still live. I shall be slowing down for some roundabout and he will step out, almost in front of me, like that fox that ran out suddenly that day in the lane and stood blinking in the beam of my headlights. He will look up and see me at the wheel. And I shall smile and wave. And he will wave back. 'What did he think he was doing?' Annie will say.

We were coming down the hill now, into the town. Around us people were walking, carrying plastic bags of shopping. Devlan pulled up at a light. 'You know, I told Rick about you, how you would never be the kind of person to do anything remotely . . .'

'Why did you get me over, then? Why did you put me through all that? What a farce!' I swallowed. 'You know there

152

was never really anything between us. You know I never even think of you these days.'

'You're wrong.' His voice had suddenly gone serious. 'Actually I've always thought it was terribly important.' He changed the subject. 'And how're the kids? How's Simon?'

I hesitated. 'Simon's fine,' I said. 'It's much better. Things have looked up a bit. We might even stay together. Actually you've been very good for us.'

'Yes?'

'Yes.'

He leaned over then and took hold of my head and kissed me. It tasted of cloth, and skin, and breathing. Not like an old man at all. More like a young man I seemed to remember from childhood. His tongue was in my mouth, huge, arching like a caterpillar. I wanted to spit it out. I was choking. He put his hands back on the wheel, at ten and two. Then he reached down, his thumb on the knob of the handbrake. 'So. Long may it continue,' he said. 'Keep up the good work.'

'Yes,' I said. I got out and shut the car door. I bent to give him a tight smile, through glass. I ran up the steps and let myself into the empty house. As I passed the hall mirror I caught sight of my reflection. My hair was sticking straight up at the crown, a caricature of revulsion or fright. It reminded me of my father. And my mouth was larger, swollen almost, as if I had been hit.

The cottage looks as it always does. I go up to the spare room under the eaves, the room I still call my study. I lie down on the bed-settee and pull the blanket up under my chin. Then I pick up the remote control from the bedside table and turn on the television. A fleet of immaculate white jet-planes is silhouetted on blue, in formation. Then a shot of dolphins leaping, one of them significantly lower than the others. A cool boyish man's voice says, 'You'll love the way we fly.' I touch a button to snap the set off.

*

153

It is New Year's Eve, just before midnight. Sean opens the champagne and pours it out into our four glasses. Mine, Deborah's, Matthew's, his own. The little bubbles rise to the surface. I look across at Matthew, but he is staring studiously into his glass. Sean leans across me to switch on the radio. 'Now, although our New Year's festivities are coming live from Vienna, New Year wouldn't be New Year without the chimes of Big Ben,' a male voice is saying.

'When do we drink?' I ask.

We look at one another.

'Is it on the first stroke or the last?'

We all grin. We don't know. 'Isn't it the last?' Deborah says.

We listen. First the chimes in their broken arpeggio. Then the slow, heavy strokes. *One, two . . .* We raise our glasses. We hold our glasses almost to our lips, waiting.

Three, four, five . . . The echoes begin to fade and music cuts in. We look at one another sheepishly. 'It must have been the first stroke,' I say.